Kay and *...*
Old friends – I *...*
you like this crazy
adventure.
Del

Knock Until
the Dog Barks

Knock Until the Dog Barks

An Adventure in Puerto Vallarta

D. E. Brobst

Strategic Book Publishing and Rights Co.

Strategic Book Publishing and Rights Co.
12620 FM 1960, Suite A4-507
Houston, TX 77065
www.sbpra.com

ISBN: 978-1-62212-373-5

Book Design by Julius Kiskis

21 20 19 18 17 16 15 14 13   1 2 3 4 5

Dedication

I am grateful for the encouragement and support of my wife,
my children and extended family,
as well as for the inspiration, energy and incredible writings
of the high school students who shared their
short stories and poems with me through the years.

Contents

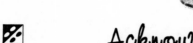

Acknowledgments

Thanks to Bill Meissner for his advice for the opening chapters,
to Mark Chirhart for being my first reader,
to Dan Schafer for being my second and third reader.
Thanks to Matthew Horning, St. John's University,
Collegeville, Minnesota graduate 2013 for the drawings
of the Doberman and the iguana.

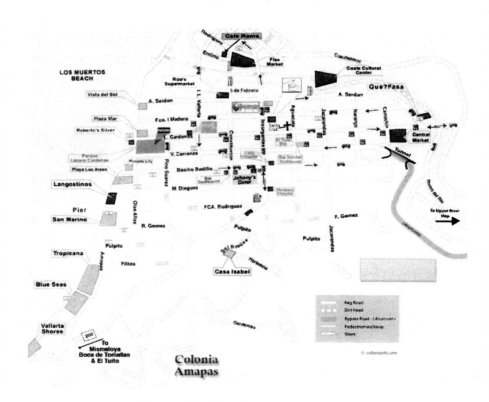

Puerto Vallarta's Romantic Zone

Chapter 1
Coco Tropical
Green Iguanas: A threatened species

Jesus Jose Martinez unfolded a white napkin from the stemmed water glass, flourished it across Candace's lap, and flashed a robust smile at yet another tiresome crowfoot blonde who caressed the air with her Coco Tropical menu. She swiveled her neck toward him. Blinked. Tossed her bleached hair side to side. Wisps of blonde blended with grey she had paid Maurice to poke through pin-holed caps at a hundred dollars per appointment, plus gratuity, twice a month at Morries of Minneapolis. This enticed Jesus to serve and flatter. She massaged the metallic-washed finish of her leather shopper Neiman Marcus purse with its hand-woven crochet accent panels as she felt for pesos to feed him

"One more, just one more margarita?" Candace asked as she fluttered her eyelids.

"Mother! All you think about is booze," daughter Emily challenged. "And men."

White Hotel Tropicana wristbands caught Jesus' eye as he escorted a third margarita to the madam's table. He secreted a smile.

"And for the lovely young lady?" He smiled widely to expose gleaming teeth. He was unsure whether more pesos lay in flattering the elder or the younger. What would his Madre say? *If I am to be true, then it is the younger. If it is to fill the family with good things, then it is the older. Juanita protect me in this my hour of need.*

Emily imagined tasting the waiter's small lips in sensuous sips. She would never admit to her friends or to her parents that she had not had sex in high school. Now in college, even at a private Catholic college, her roommate suspected she was still a virgin. Nothing more needed to be revealed to anyone. This near-escape of losing her virginity to a St. John's freshman drove her to *Puerto Vallarta* where she could experiment. Mother paid the fare.

Jesus' tips were small—his desire was immense. From four tables he needed to extract pesos enough to spread among Father, Mother and two siblings, yet save enough for Juanita. A calico cat nuzzled his ankle. Jesus brushed it aside. The cat moaned.

"Emily?" Candace admonished. "Stop undressing our waiter. Would you like a Virgin Mary?" Candace's eyes slipped above the rim of her margarita. Granules of salt stuck to her mascara-laden eyelids.

"Mother! You are so crude. When I was five, it was Shirley Temples. Now I'm twenty and you," she stopped and gasped. "Now you embarrass me by ordering bloody virgins. I am, Mother, capable of ordering for myself." Emily slipped her middle finger beneath the white Tropicana Hotel rubber band on her wrist. "Waiter," she commanded. "Bring me a rum and Coke. Two shots of rum, please." She smiled at her mother.

Candace ignored her. She wanted no part of yet another scene with Emily. Tilting her head she drank the remains of her margarita.

Barry asked Jesus Jose to steady him on his way from Coco Tropical's half-price happy-hour drinks to a private table. Jesus Jose escorted Barry down two steps to the restaurant's most remote bayside table. Candace and Emily sipped drinks.

"It's Max." Barry looked up at Jesus. "Max. Max like your former Emperor, and exactly like the restaurant Maximillian. You know the restaurant Maximillian? It's just an easy jog from here, you know? We should jog and go," Barry said.

"Yes, of course, *amigo.* Everyone knows of Maximilian's. It is not still happy hour here, *amigo.* But on this day—this day only I will bring you two for the price of one. But I cannot go now to Maximilian's. Another time maybe?"

"You must call me Max, *amigo.* If only you knew the English idiom better, you might know how delicious two-for-the-price-of-one sounds." Barry would never have been this bold in Minnesota. He would never have dared to think of such a *ménage a trois* in high school After Crosier, Saint John's had immersed him in liberal education. Rather than learning to be tolerant of deviant views, Barry learned to deceive.

"Bring me two margaritas rocas. Salt and two limes."

Jesus ignored Barry's raised eyebrows. He was too familiar with intrigues that required him to deliver service as well as spirits to faces everywhere in the restaurant. He delivered male-to-male, female-to-male, male-to-female, female-to-female—never flinching or raising an eyebrow as long as tips were generous.

Having watched hundreds of hours of television, Jesus memorized professional basketball, football, and hockey team names. He memorized teams alphabetically by league without a hint of an accent. Since many American tourists were from the Midwest, Jesus gave especial effort to their teams. He could not know the irony of their prayers for victory. Jesus could recite team names in perfect ESPN English: Timberwolves, Vikings, Packers, Bulls, Bears, Blackhawks, Pistons. Tips squeezed from double margaritas garnished with bits of sports banter came to him generously along with high fives and slaps on the back. It paid to offer two for one.

"Hey!" Candace summoned with a twist of lime pulp slipping from her lip. She pointed her double-jointed diamond-ringed forefinger toward him, flipped her bleached blonde hair with a lazy shake of her head, and slurred, "Heyzeus. Sweetheart. *La quenta, por favor.* Emily, Emily, you, you look so, so pale. I only meant please bring the check. Oh," Candace put her hand on Emily's shoulder. "It is the eyes, the eyes of the handsome Heyzeus. No, no. He's your no-no." She thrust her head backwards and laughed.

Jesus thrust his pelvis toward mother's and daughter's eyes. Thin-to-the-bone with a matador's elongated muscles, Jesus' bronze arms rippled from blazing white polo sleeves stitched with the Coco Tropical palm tree logo. Black hair shimmered in the spots of light projected from incandescents.

"I am pleased to pleasure you." *Tips,* he thought. *I must work for tips for the house and me.* He smiled at Emily. His tight-at-the-crotch black pants enticed Candace's and Emily's eyes to swim the waves from the shine of his shoes to the white of his teeth to the sheen of his hair. He brushed his hip close to Candace's elbow. With a flourish he unsheathed the check from the apron pocket between his navel and crotch.

"For the beautiful ladies, I give a discount from my own wages that I share with my own mother." He knelt like a matador before the bull, the check pointed from his fingertips toward Candice's neck. He posed for the final plunge of the sword. Bartender nodded to manager. Candace fumbled in her Versace Canyon Denim Croc handbag.

Intrigued by the sideshow, yet knowing he knew them, Barry averted his eyes. His stomach churned. Daughter so much like the mother. No. Not here. Not now. How? Why? Pool. Chase had arranged the pool job.

"They have money," Chase had admonished him. "But beware of Mother and don't let them know about us." Barry needed summer money and Wayzata's prolific pool owners provided opportunities for friends of the wealthy. "Don't mention me or St. John's to Mother," Chase advised.

White rubber wristbands blazed on sun-tanned wrists. The week's Tropicana wristbands were white—unnatural in *Puerto Vallarta*. Brown sugar sand. Pesos brown. Pelicans brown. Cats brown. Lovers brown.

Jesus delivered Candace's check in one hand like a *picador*, the other dipping dramatically in compliment as he approached the grinning bartender.

Barry turned to the two women. He raised his right index finger. "The check, please, amigo." He pinched a 100-peso note between his left hand thumb and finger.

Jesus smiled, plucked the 100-peso note from Barry's thumb and forefinger, pirouetted on tiptoe around Barry's table and strutted to the bar.

"There's always more for great service," Barry whispered to himself.

"Emily, dahling. Our waiter was so so so so. Tomorrow night we must come back. Archie's succulent ribs can wait." Candace giggled, unaware of anything or anyone other than herself. She flopped her hand onto Emily's shoulder to steady herself.

"Mother!" Emily admonished.

"Please. Let me pleasure you with dessert." Jesus smiled.

Candace rolled her eyes. A grain of salt stung her eye. "Excuse me!" She rushed from the table, her lips congealing as if she were sucking a lime. She samba-swayed to the restroom.

"I'll have a Coke with rum and lime," Emily said as she brushed her elbow against Jesus' thigh. She flicked her tongue, cupped her palm as if cradling a large banana, slid it toward her lips.

Jesus felt a sting creep from where the imprint of her blue-blaze eyes burned his like tequila. He glanced toward the sky above the restaurant patio, made a mental sign of the cross as he approached the bar.

The bartender grinned and nodded. They had worked together for several weeks, ever since the rainy season. The bartender glanced toward the back of the restaurant, where the manager chatted with a customer. Knowing that he and Jesus might divide a big tip, the bartender tripled the rum in the Coke, poured doubly generous shots of Absolut Citron into the Coke, and winked at Jesus.

Jesus Jose dreamed of cooler climes and fewer hours of delivering pesos to those who waited for his wages behind *Puerto Vallarta's* open windows. Jesus Jose imagined flying the night sky after work where he would meld with the moon's splashing light. If only . . . if only there were angels' wings to waft him skyward. The sound of retching destroyed his reverie. He sensed rather than heard the sound of splash, blinked uncontrollably, gasped as the stench of vomit billowed. He looked down. He saw a tongue flick like a plump snake the instant before more vomit spewed as the once beautiful blonde slipped sideways on her chair. Strings of partially digested cheese, a fleck of red snapper, and brown Coke clung to the orchid flower on her Geox sandals.

Jesus Jose knelt beside her. He would never become accustomed to wiping the feet of *gringos*. He was accustomed to the stench of vomit. He was not afraid to kneel. Sometimes it brought peace if not pesos. He reached discreetly into Emily's lap to remove her cloth napkin and wiped clean her toes, shoes, and ankles. With the raised-hand flare of a *toreador* summoning the sword, Jesus summoned the bus boy who wiped the puddle away with swoops of a bar towel.

Candace stumbled to the table. Seemingly stable, she smoothed the back of her blouse to tuck it in with one hand, waved the other for balance.

Jesus thought, *Why do they eat and pay and drink and eat so much to vomit and pay to eat and pay and drink to eat so much only to vomit?* He bowed as he delivered Candace's check. The bartender grinned and opened a bottle of tequila.

Thursday night's shift over, Jesus Jose, thinking of embracing pesos flowing from patrons' hands more quickly than the tequila they gulped, could not wash servitude's aftertaste from his mouth. A beer with Clamato might cleanse mouth and mind, but tonight he enjoyed the lingering taste of the blonde's tips he had touched. Jesus, elbows pinioned to the bar, propped his head in his hands. Minutes metered his day. It was time for this night to release him from bondage to *el Norte* dollars. Weekend would bring day shifts at the Tropicana Hotel. The bartender pinched Jesus' cheek, patted him on the back three times. More pats would not be manly.

After work Jesus Jose escaped to the Malecon where he could listen to the waves splash while he gazed at the childlike sculpture of couples gazing out to sea. He did not know that the title of the sculpture he loved was *"La Nostalgia."* He knew little of romance. In grade school, a few blocks from *Puerto Vallarta's* old town square, he had learned of the romance between the artist Barquet and his wife who came to this spot to enjoy the beautiful *Puerto Vallarta* sunsets. Jesus gazed at the Barquet sculptures as dreams curdled in his stomach. When he was a child, he had dreamed of whens: when childhood was behind him, when he was old enough, when he could support himself, when he could choose destinations, when he could make dreams come true. Suddenly he sensed the whens had to be answered now. Now blonde and mother assaulted his senses. Would the three hundred pesos of this night's work be enough to discover answers?

Candace and Emily, full of lust for Jesus, dreamed of paying to lie with him. Jesus would wait tables, strut, dance, pose, demean himself for pesos, but to be paid for sex was beyond his Latino understanding. He feared that Mother Mary and all the Saints would slip into the folds of his soul and burn it if he had such thoughts of sex with the blondes. Juanita would disown him. She warned that blondes were the Devil's bed partners. If a blonde from the north wrapped him in her arms and whispered siren songs, Jesus would cross himself even in his naked need for sex and implore Juanita to staunch the swelling of his lust.

Coco Tropical: Anonymous Internet Posts

Loved our waiter. He was very knowledgeable, funny and entertaining. Food was good, great atmosphere. They were having Greek night, the time we were there, but you could order off their regular menu as well, (which we did), but the belly dancer was great, very talented.

Chapter 2

Café de Olla

Human's name: Iguanas don't

If you have a name in Puerto Vallarta, it is wise to tell it to the iguana and to no one else. Jesus Jose knew this. Few others were as wise. Barry had slipped away to Puerto Vallarta after Chase's wedding. The wedding's chill bit his flesh more intensely than Minnesota's winter wind. He had heard of the filming of *The Night of the Iguana* and of its stars Taylor, Burton and director Huston. He had eaten at Archie's Wok because a dancer at the Gay Nineties bar on Minneapolis' Hennepin Avenue had told him that's where Walter Huston's former personal chef made more delicious ribs than one would ever encounter in the bar. Barry considered himself a sophisticated recent graduate of St. John's University in Collegeville, Minnesota. It was a university in name only because it offered a Master's Degree in Theology—nothing else. But he wondered how long a restaurant such as Archie's Wok could exist on a reputation decades old.

Barry felt superior to cruise ship tourists who bargained for trinkets at the flea market, where they paid too many pesos because they couldn't determine how to subtract a zero from a peso note to approximate costs in what they called real money. He would not admit that on his spring break visit he had breathed hard and heavy, felt the sweat drip from his armpits as he haggled over the price of two three-inch ceramic copulating pigs. Chase had paid for the trip, but his parents had insisted that he do his week with them in Wayzata. Barry's sweat smelled sweet to him when he sensed he had swindled the Mexican out of five pesos. Chase might be proud. Now Barry longed for Archie's ribs.

Barry curried favor from rambling street dogs by feeding them leftover ribs while ignoring men holding hands on stools next to him at Choco Banana's street bar. He was neither racist nor homophobic, nor was he xenophobic except when it came to eating escargot or speaking French. He bragged of knowing that the Hundred Years War was between Great Britain and France, but he would never eat Brie. He would never reveal that his grandfather was born in an unheated upstairs bedroom on a farm in Hayfield, Minnesota. He coveted the sound of Blooming Prairie. That would have been a town for ancestors he could have borne.

Behind gated door of 110 *Miramar* "Rooms to Let," where a half-block away clanking diesel bus engines belched carbon clouds that engulfed horny taxi honks *Latino* tunes blared and basses thumped. Barry suffered from a relationship with a former Edina High School tennis star who had married. His desire to seduce anyone-whose-name-he-could-not-remember at Andale's at *Olas Altas* in the small hours of days rose within him each morning. After showering, he sniffed the sleeve of his wrinkled Saint John's University red polo as he searched for a scent he did not recognize. Sensing odor neither male nor female, he inhaled. His stomach grumbled that it was time for lunch at Freddy's Toucan, a short invigorating jog from *Miramar*. Barry often slaked his thirst for sex with coffee and French toast crusted with almonds, raisins and fruit of the day at Freddy's.

Charming in a Midwestern way, Barry would say "Pardon me," when the house cleaner, if she rapped unexpectedly and unlocked his door before he could slip from naked to boxers to say, "I'll just be a *jalapeno*. I'm so sorry for sleeping too long." Steeping in the nude heat at Miramar-with-kitchenette where smooth breezes excited his privates, he grinned—recalling his mother's shriek when as a teenager, he had poked his forefinger through the slit in his boxer shorts when she woke him for school. His current roommate may or may not be amused. He liked to be called Queen by friends when he growled and snarled at them to make them laugh.

At number 110 *Miramar, Puerto Vallarta, Jalisco,* Mexico, Barry would neglect to place a few pesos on the pillow as gratuity for the house cleaner's work. Queen always escaped before the cleaner's arrival. He didn't want to be discovered or uncovered. Barry's mother, Sharon, had told Barry that he should always remember to tip, but after the towel had slid from his waist to his toes when he opened the door a discreet six inches, he held out hope that the cleaning woman would at least smile. Her eyes were a cornucopia of contrasts. He didn't know whether her eyes revealed surprise, intrigue or a curse. She knew no English. He knew little Spanish. Following his residence at Crosier Prep followed by Saint John's University's requirement of two years of study of a world language, he still had not mastered Spanish. "*Hola on.*" She slammed the door.

His youth had been filled with the sound of slammed doors. It took years for Barry to begin to decipher why his dad was so angry and so impulsive. Something had happened in Vietnam that was never talked about. When Barry was fifteen, he made a dangerous, emotional decision. Yes, he knew there would be consequences, but he had no idea what they would be. His dad, Rick, and his mother, Sharon, were red-faced and shouting. Half-eaten dinners wobbled on the table when his father stomped from the kitchen to the drop-leaf dining table.

"Bills!" His father thrust a fistful of paper into her face. "You've been hiding these!" He drew back his arm as if he were going to smash Sharon's face with the wads of paper. "We have no money!" With both hands Barry grabbed his father's arm. His father had never touched him in anger. He only threatened. Rick flung his free arm around Barry's neck in a headlock. "I've seen enough of your face! Don't you ever touch me again!"

Barry was supposed to have learned a little of humility, a bit of Catechism and some Latin along with Spanish after his dad delivered him without explanation to Crosier Prep in Onamia, Minnesota, and drove away. Barry studied hard, earned outstanding grades and won a scholarship to St. John's University, with the implied promise that he would someday enter seminary.

Barry's image of Brother Smoley, his Crosier Prep English teacher, who had dubbed him Jarhead when he responded to a question by quipping that William Shakespeare was born in Avon, Minnesota, invaded his mind. Jarhead had stuck to his classmates' lips. Ever after, Barry dreamed of nailing Brother Smoley's balls to a stump and pushing him over while chanting, "All's well that ends well. That's what I know of William."

Barry's date for the Crosier Prep Homecoming Dance thought the nickname Jarhead was cute. "Jarhead, the punch in my glass is empty," she giggled. Barry's tuxedo coat's inner pocket was wide and deep, a perfect pouch for the fifth of Smirnoff. He poured all into the punch bowl with his left hand while engaging the eyes of the head chaperone in Beowulfish banter. She was oblivious to the deceptions of good students, as well as of those of whom she should be suspicious. On this night Barry glowed.

He grasped his date's hand, smiled, kissed her on the cheek and whispered in her ear, "Shall I compare thee to a summer's day?" He paused and stared dreamily into her wet eyes. She appealed to him in that moment. Her fingers gripped his with too much tension, as if there was an energy there, which he neither wanted to accept nor reject. "Thee art my sweet illiterate?"

Intoxicated from the Coco Tropical encounter, Barry abandoned his plan to have his favorite breakfast of French toast with raisins, crusted almonds and mangos at Freddy's Toucan restaurant. He was still hung over from the effects of too much tequila and the intrigue of spying on Chase's mother and sister. He enjoyed watching action from afar and imagining a variety of scenarios and climaxes. His creative writing at Crosier, however, was not applauded, but the staff of the College of Saint Benedict's creative magazine *Studio One* published his short story "A Broken Ego." He based the story on the conversations he and Chase had shared late nights after swimming and studying. They had a blood-brother agreement that neither would share any of their thoughts and views with anyone—ever. Chase complained of his parents having too much money. Rick told the story of his father's dumping him at Crosier Prep. Both knew that their parents would never get along, so they made a pact to hide their friendship from them. Chase had a brilliant idea.

"I'll get some of my parents' money transferred from their fists to yours. How would you like a summer job tending their pool and gardens in the summer?"

After the girl's splash of vomit and Chase's mother's slurred speech, Barry knew he wanted to know more of why they were here. Why here? Here after the wedding? Family here? Yes. Sure. Chase here? No. Chase would do anything to escape them. He wouldn't honeymoon here. White wristbands. Tropicana. Not wanting to risk Candace recognizing him from his pool and gardening days, fearing that she might recall that he had never delivered filters to her pool, he still wanted to discover why they were in *Puerto Vallarta.*

Hotel Tropicana's wristbands are white this week. Cafe American near the Tropicana invited couples. Robust, inexpensive coffee aromas wafted there. Petite stools accommodated slender cheeks. They would not stop there.

Get there early, Barry thought. Choco Banana. *Desaylnos Completos* breakfast banner invited guests from the wrought iron fence enclosing a four-by-eight-foot sidewalk eating area where they had to pass. *Yes, they would have to pass. Perch on a stool—a stool in a shadowy corner beneath tile roof.* There the view of *Calle Amapas* would be undisturbed. Tropicana guests always walked *Calle Amapas* to the eateries. His intuition told him they would not walk the beach in the morning. They would not want to get sand on their pedicured toes so early in the day. Yes, that's where they would pass. He stood unsteadily. He loved the Romantic Zone. No need for a cab. No need for directions. Every enticement to after-hours excitement was within walking distance.

Barry dressed. Tossed his Minnesota Twins baseball hat to the bed. *What a fool,* he thought. *Logo gives me away.* He reached for the red and navy Saint John's University baseball hat. He recoiled from the imagined burn. *Stupid. Really stupid.* Somewhere, somewhere in his carelessly strewn wrinkled boxer shorts, and shirts emblazoned with SJU logos, he dug until he found an innocuous baseball cap he had purchased in Dayton's department store at Crossroads Mall in Saint Cloud. He slipped into khaki cargo shorts and a t-shirt emblazoned with Corona's blue and yellow label. Now he felt like Everyman south of the border.

Barry knew he could course unnoticed through *Puerto Vallarta's* streets where some were on a mission to get laid by either sex; some were on a crusade to get laid by their own. Everyone seemed to be stalking something, something promising their escape from destruction. Partners were publically discreet in *Puerto Vallarta*. Barry, who had never kissed a person in public, was too nervous to wear Nike tennis shoes because he thought they might cause an observer to notice the logo and remember it and him. He slipped into white sneakers.

He pulled the nondescript baseball hat close to cover his eyebrows. This cool morning invited Barry to jog slowly to avoid raising a sweat. He eased down *Miramar* past the flea market building with its dark and cool interior. Careful not to twist an ankle on uneven cobblestones he stepped onto the Malecon. His stomach lurched a bit from the night's after-acid tequila swells, but he felt clean in white hat and sneakers. He focused on the irregular cobblestones. A sprained ankle would be nasty. His jog from *Miramar* to *Guerrero* had been easy, left to *Calle Mananoros* to the church and down *Calle Independencia* to the Malecon where an easy jog led to the pier, with a final trot up *Pulpito* to Choco Banana on *Amapas*.

With a sigh and a fresh smile for the Choco bartender, Barry ordered a glass of fresh-squeezed orange juice. Sugar infused his brain. He glanced at the money exchange booth across the street to see the day's exchange rate. The rate rarely fluctuated, but he checked it because of impatience and anxiety: 10.8 pesos American. He glanced up Amapas Calle. Had he guessed wrong? No. They had to stay at the Tropicana—white wristband. *Why are they in Puerto Vallarta? Mysterious. College. Minnesota. Chase never talked about them. Got me the pool job. Kept me away. Memory. Something to do with senior year? The bridge? No. Not that. They could not have known of the Brother's caution. Not there. No one knew of that.* Voices disturbed his reverie.

On the three feet of corner sidewalk Choco Banana did not occupy, two men in tight-white shorts nodded to the women.

"No, Mother, I don't," Barry heard her say, "I don't want something nutritious."

"But Emily. It will be good for us. Too much tequila."

"No! Father said Cafe de Olla. And it's not far. I looked at the map. Choco Banana is not breakfast."

"Oh, Emily. I don't know what to do with you. You, you always fuss—frustrate me. Okay. Okay. Olla it is. You do have the map, don't you?

"Jesus! I don't need it. Follow me. It's easy to find."

"Emily. For Chrissakes, don't swear."

"It's on *Basilio Badillo*. How do you say?"

"Emily. It makes no difference. Nobody but waiters understand English, much less pidgin Spanish. Just give me the map."

Barry slapped a thirty peso on the bar to cover his orange juice plus a small tip. He did not want to be remembered. He loitered until they rounded the corner. No need to follow. He knew Café de Olla always had a long breakfast line—same as Freddy's Toucan. Both served food as fresh and tasty as any served at Archie's Wok or Coco Tropical. As Barry turned the corner on *Basilio Badillo* the squat Mexican woman clad in a blaze-white cotton polo squeezed oranges today as she had each of the months during the tourist season.

Tourists forfeit fifteen pesos to sip fresh squeezed orange juice. Nudging another orange from the mesh sack into the squeezer, she smiles a toothless *"Buenos dias, amigo."*

There they stood. Young blonde, feet spread, a stance a matador would find challenging to assume, raises her arm, stabs her finger toward the open window of the cafe.

Emily? I know. I know the hair. They—here. Perspiration. Wipe. Damn. No sweat.

The Empress of 1357 Cargill Drive, Wayzata, Minnesota grasped Emily's wrist in an attempt to wrest her from the unfolding Cafe de Olla scene. Candace bumped hips with the chef cooking breakfast steaks on the sidewalk charcoal grill. He reached out to pat her buttocks, but Candace stuck fast to her daughter.

Emily grasped Candace's wrist with her free hand and the two performed the *Danse Macabre*. Celebration laughter swelled inside Cafe de Olla.

Six thirty-something men ogled a twenty-something waiter clad in a purple, palm-leafed tropical shirt knotted below his hairless nipples punctuated by a six-pack of abs. Margarita rocks clinked in glasses on the tray he balanced on one hand above his head. He began to croon, "Happy birthday. Happy birthday to you," as he deftly dipped the tray of margaritas to the table. From his left hand he flourished a pewter plate he had disguised behind his back. His right hand unveiled a red napkin concealing an eight-inch oblong object lying prostrate on the pewter plate. Left palm under plate, he pirouetted, bent and flexed his buttocks to uproarious applause and guffaws from the six. He flipped the red napkin from the tray with a magician's flair and draped it over the birthday boy's head. He slipped his hand under two three-inch doughnut holes attached to the eight-inch *éclair* into the cup of his hand. With utmost care and precision he suspended the entire concoction between index finger and thumb inches above the birthday boy's lips.

Birthday boy, shirtless, waxed and bronzed, knowing this was all his, gazed dreamily at the pastry. The waiter tipped it toward the boy's contorted lips. Cameras flashed. Roaring shouts and hand claps erupted from the six who had ordered the birthday present. Waiter squeezed the *éclair*. Sweet cream oozed from the tip. Laughter and applause erupted for the five conspirators as cream dripped into the birthday boy's upturned mouth.

Candace Cargill-Maximillian dug her fingernails into Emily's wrist. "Disgusting!" She clutched Emily's arm. "Thank God your father isn't here to witness this. . . this, this, this," she stammered.

"Mother, dammit. Let go of me. "

"Emily! Do not. You do not talk to me that way. Your father. My God, your father would disown you!"

Blood from the half-moon cuts of her mother's nails trickled from her forearm as Emily broke her mother's grasp. "I hate this. This control. Leave me alone!" She, turned and walked rapidly down *Basilio Badillo,* past the white brick and iron-barred windows of the elementary school.

Flames of fury tightened Candace's sun-scorched wrinkles. "Stop! Emily. Stop. Stop this instant," she shouted.

Tourists, lined up like bulbs of Christmas lights outside Café de Olla, gasped.

Candace flung her sandals into the air with the same precision of her husband's flipping Ralph Lauren boxers from foot to towel hook as she charged down the street.

Candace had been too young to reap the benefits of Minnesota's Title IX law that forced schools to equalize the number of sports between men and women. Eyota High School in southeastern Minnesota had a track team for boys. Candace was one of few women among the forty-seven seniors at Eyota High School, a place tucked between "Rochister" as the locals referred to it and the Mississippi river bluffs, who dreamed of competing in track and field. She could run. She had learned early in her experience how to relay. She could pass a baton from boy to boy with no drops. Boys she could hurdle. High jumps were never a problem. Pole vaults made her grin. She could bend the studs' poles with one dropping lip. She stunned boys by standing on the sidelines in her tight knits that were cold in winter and hot in summer—hotter in fall playoffs.

Eleanor, Candace's mother, having made one of very few indiscriminate decisions during a promising career as a medical secretary at the Rochester's Mayo Clinic, paid cash for a Chevy Camaro convertible as a high school graduation gift after her father sold a prized Black Angus. Candace's convertible caught Jules' eye when she drove with the top down by Eyota High School where Jules taught agriculture and maintained the school grounds. After he was elected president of the Rochester Chapter of the Isaac Walton League, republican politicos relied on him to deliver the vote in state and national elections. He delivered. Eleanor dated him for six months, settled and married.

Teenage Candace also delivered. She delivered her father's political posters up and down each of Eyota's ten square blocks laid out by Oscar Madison in 1843. After all posters were delivered, she strutted into Eyota's lone hardware store owned by Robert Madison, whose sign advertised Master of Nuts and Bolts. He knew that Candace was no fool. She smiled. Shifted hip to tip as she had seen Marilyn do in *"Some Like it Hot."* Robert squinted—peered through latticed eyes at Candace's cleavage. Candace delivered more than most in Eyota could imagine. Eyota jocks dropped passes while dreaming of dropping their drawers with Candace in the bench seats of their fathers' Fords.

Eyota's pool hall's failed jocks faulted sons for latching eyes on Candace instead of the ball. Forgetful of the stink of their losses to teams from towns too small to merit dots on mind maps, towns such as Elgin, Millville and Dover, they filled their bellies with pickled eggs, beef jerky and bullshit about their high school heroics in the Cougar's Den—Eyota's beer joint. After football losses, they shared beers and smarts of what they would have done with Candace if they had been her age.

Candace reclaimed and renamed herself Candace Cargill-Maximillian when she married into the Cargill-Maximillian fortune. Buxom, smart, knowing she deserved privilege, and having a social climber's body to succeed, she seduced Daniel on a private Halloween hay ride she had won in a Cargill drawing at the Olmsted County Fair.

"Who needs a college education?" Candace was quoted in the *Rochester Post Bulletin* June report of the Eyota Days Celebration where she rode the float commemorating her having been voted Mrs. Eyota. "I made it. Anyone can make it if I, from little Eyota, could." She sweated through the July heat of the parade in the last month of her second pregnancy and delivered a second Cargill-Maximillian that they christened Emily after the great grandmother of the dynasty's great, great grandmother.

Café de Olla: Anonymous Internet Post
Café de Olla doesn't look like much from the outside. There are several glitzier looking places in this restaurant row area of the city. But our hotel had recommended it and we decided to give it a try (especially after seeing that some of these glitzier places offered "specialties," such as fettuccine alfredo along with Mexican food). For our one night in Mexico, we wanted something more authentic. And that's what we got. A very charming restaurant with a pleasant interior (bigger than it looks from the outside). Delcious chips with spicy salsas. More chips with fantastic fresh guacamole. Tasty margaritas. Entrees were good but the appetizers were actually a little better. Dessert was a nice cake made even better with chocolate sauce and ice cream. Complimentary house-made tequila when we finished our meal was a really nice touch.

Friday: Iguanas lay eggs. Leave them and do not return. When iguana babies hatch, they grow up without care from their parents.

Emily looked over her shoulder to see her mother running toward her. Emily could fly across cobblestones as deftly as her mother pursued men, money and status. Emily burst into a run—tears flowing freely. Gasping for air, her flailing arms knocked aside a child who stood with open arms—his mother lurking in the shadows. Chiclets and tiny toy turtles with skinny necks and wobbly feet that wiggled at the mere touch of hand or whisper of breeze spilled into the street from the box the tot held in his tiny hands. "Five pesos?" He begged with empty hands and glistening eyes.

Emily stopped. She walked to this no-bigger-than-a-fireplug child. His skin gleamed in the sun. Frantic for pesos, she dug a twenty-peso note from her Versace clutch purse, scooped spilled gum and turtles from cobblestones into her hands as deftly as a child playing a game of jacks. She turned again to see if Mother followed. Seeing nothing, Emily dumped Chiclets, turtles and pesos into the child's outstretched hands held in practiced supplication beneath chocolate eyes.

Hot sun firing her flesh, sweat beading on her brow, Emily stopped to survey the street. There was no sign of her mother. Nerves shredding thoughts, she sucked in the humid air, turned and sprinted toward the river.

She charged through the day—sensing, hoping, and despairing. *No one ever leaves me alone. She never trusts me. I want to get away. To be me. Mother should be wrapped in cellophane and hawked at fairs as the cheap confection that she is. Father was always marking me with his name. Bragging and reminding me that he's paying my tuition, but gave me no choice of a college. Both he and mother insisted that I attend a small, private college. Mother tries to make me over in her image. Somebody help. Chase told me about trust. He meant money. I have no use for that kind of trust.*

Somewhere among cruise ship women shoppers, and their khaki-clad mates, Emily fled. She trailed tourist throngs through the flea market while they haggled and marveled over mirrors framed in patina-painted tin offered at half-price today just for *amigos*. A blonde flashing her newly purchased silver bracelet nudged her husband, "Oh wouldn't that purse make a perfect gift for my sister when she comes for her birthday in November to stay in the guest house?"

"Um?" he murmured. "I've never been fond of beaded purses."

Emily stood between the couple and the ceramic turtles strangled by their necks on a wire. She glanced right, left, behind, afraid that Mother might reappear. She prayed she had given up the chase and had gone back to the Tropicana. On the second floor of the crowded flea market she elbowed her way through waves of gray and blue-gray hair, clutches of towheads tethered to blonde mothers, all lighted by bulbs hanging on thin wires. 12:20 p.m. Two hours. Punish her with worry. But *Puerto Vallarta* is a small cage. Bandaris Bay bars the way north and west. Sierra Madre guards the bay's back. Where to flee? Where to run? Emily wasn't certain how long she should punish her mother. *Overnight would scare her more than enough*, she thought.

Writhing through trinket-filled aisles, Emily smelled the simmer of tomatoes, the waft of cilantro, the sear of charcoal. She elbowed a bargaining cruise shipper aside as she stumbled down the steps to the flea market's street level. She squinted to right herself as she emerged from the shadowy light of the flea market to the brilliantly sunlit street. Right, the rushing traffic; left, the sloping street to the bay. Everywhere a cage.

Buses belched passengers, exhaled diesel smoke, and rattle-roared over the *Cuale* Bridge on *Libertad*. Emily crossed under the bridge where she had seen feral cats curled in the sand and iguana lazing in the canopy above. She knew that Mother would retrace the steps they had taken together the day before when they had stopped to pet a Calico. *No. No. No. I will make Mother worry. I will make Candace care. I will show Mother I can be me. I can party all night while she worries.* Her wrists ached. *Blood. Mother made me bleed. I will make her sorry.* She stooped to pet the cat. A hand on her shoulder startled her.

"Forgive . . ." was all Emily heard as she whirled.

"Stop," echoed as Emily dodged venders along *Rio Caule. Run. God I hurt.*

Candace collapsed on the steps leading from the Cuale Bridge to the river. Folded her arms as if she could become a shell. No more. No more chasing. Chase honeymooning in Aruba. No more chasing Emily. The cat rubbed its back on her legs. Candace reached to stroke its tail. It hissed and spat at her, and bounded to the corrugated street vendors' roofs that shielded plastic rosaries, sequined velvet sombreros, among Corona ponchos from sun and infrequent rain. Candace stood. Enough. She'd had enough. She shaded her eyes, and squinted at the disappearing Calico.

Chapter 3
Tropicana Hotel
Friday: Iguanas are diurnal.

*T*hey are also cold-blooded, which means they do not produce their own body heat. If it is cold, the iguana is cold. To raise body temperature, green iguanas bask in the sun to soak the sun's heat from rocks or tree canopy.

Chase curved his legs around the heat of Kellie's buttocks. Warmth oozed from the sexual fire of these two who had recently married in the Minneapolis Church of the Blessed Atonement. Kellie lay dreaming of having been recently filled with a fiery arrow dipped in warm oils. Her muscles twitched with the warmth of Chase's flesh nestled in the crook of her knees. She felt the press of penis beneath her buttocks. She sighed, hugged her pillow. Chase rolled to his back, grasped his erection with four fingers and thumb. Tempted toward masturbation, he fought the pounding of his conscience. *It is now we. Not lonely me.*

A full moon burst behind a cloud while he lay entangled with Kellie, his new Mrs. He, Chase, her new Mr. Mr. and Mrs., 'til death never parting. His stomach tensed as he fought back wriggling worms of nausea. Mr. and Mrs. inundated his consciousness summoning the same taste of shame as when his mother had stolen the privacy of his masturbating. He had

24

always been careful to make no sound. He lay in bed fingering his erection as he listened for voices from the living room. Hearing no voices, no television, no rattling of water pipes, no flushing noises in the night heat, he thrust the sheet from the tent made above his groin. He closed his eyes and conjured images of Greek orgies. Aphrodite's breasts. Apollo's curls. A stab of light split the images into a phosphorescent mass. His mother's astringent voice made him shiver. Cupping both hands over his exposed genitalia, he fish-flipped to his stomach. He fought the rise of nausea, swallowed, and buried his head in his pillow. Dear God, he uttered in silent desperation, "Make this a dream, and I will never do it again."

"Chase?"

Every muscle rigid, he prayed she would dissolve into wallpaper. Nails raked his shoulder. He smothered his face in the pillow.

"I know you aren't sleeping. I heard you groaning." With one hand on top of his shoulder, Candace bent to kiss the back of his neck. "Nightmares can grow into night terrors, honey"

Chase flipped from back to front and threw open the sheet to expose his erection. "This is your nightmare. It's my dream." He laughed.

Inhaling Pacific breezes, Chase nestled his hand onto the small of Kellie's back. He felt the smooth warmth of her calm, but the savage roar of waves drew him to the balcony. Kellie's blonde hair shimmered in the moonlight. How much he wanted to touch her, draw her to him, enter the place that promised to quiet his soul. Her sweet murmur of sleep calmed him until he felt his erection throb. Rolling to the bed's edge, he reached to the floor to find where he had slipped out of his Speedo after their evening swim. The nylon was cold. This Speedo was a gift from his best friend who had refused to be his best man. Its red and white stars on royal blue were the same pattern as Chase and his swim team buddies had worn at St. John's University. It had just enough fabric to cover what they wanted girls to uncover. Chase's best friend had taught Chase that he should cup his hand under his penis when he slipped into his Speedo. Then the head of his penis would stand up rather than fold down.

"Women and gays like that," his friend had laughed.

"And you?" Chase laughed.

They slapped hands and grinned. "Let's go kick some ass. You dive a 9.9 and I'll anchor."

Doors are thin at the Tropicana. Elevators offer no escape or alarms. Children few. Honeymooners nearly nonexistent. Chase and Kellie were among the few Minnesotans who stayed at the Tropicana who had actually read and discussed *The Great Gatsby*. Those who understood were even fewer. Fitzgerald's *The Great Gatsby* was required reading in many of Minnesota's high school and college English classes. Few Minnesotans admired the rich. If you drove a Cadillac or a Saab in Minnesota, you were eyed suspiciously. Fitzgerald's Nick was both hero and victim. He was smitten with Gatsby's wealth just as Chase's mother was smitten with Rochester's Pill Hill mansions when seen from the window of her father's Ford. Every time he drove her to Rochester to admire clothing at Dayton's that they could not afford, they toured Pill Hill. Everyone in rural Olmsted County knew Pill Hill and the Libby's image of an ear-of-corn water tower. Candace's dad told the same joke on each trip into and out of Rochester. You know they are demolishing the tower? "Don't start," she grimaced. "I know. It has a worm in it."

Freshman year at Saint John's University, Chase had been required to read *Giovanni's Room*. Liberal studies were meant to open conservative minds to liberal views. Professor Brother Onan had concluded that, since most of his first-year boys were naive, they should read and discuss without blush, fuss or remorse, James *Baldwin's Giovanni's Room.* Chase would never forget the last lines when Giovanni tossed paper pieces into the wind. Would he? Kellie never understood why Gatsby had to be blown away on a pneumatic mattress. His success, his charisma, and his opulent life left nothing to her imagining of a heavenly romance.

Chase and Kellie's honeymoon had been the gift of a great uncle from Fargo, North Dakota. He had fathered no children. He chose Chase as his surrogate son. The great uncle's advice came every Saturday morning in a phone call ever since Chase could remember being able to speak. Candace had always forced him to reply to the last few sentences to the great hoped-for benefactor. All Chase could ever think to say was, "Love you. Bye."

Recollections of Saturday phone calls echoed in Chase's mind. *Silly boy. Liar. Pretender. Wish I didn't wish you were dead and buried in North Dakota so I didn't have to pretend love.* Chase's heart pounded. Hands slick with sweat, he craved to creep into Kellie's warmth to quiet the roar within him. Turning to see if she still slept, he was drawn to the door. His anxiety of being the good son raced his heart.

Good son's goodness was to beg money from a father who had too much and never wanted for anything ever, and never breathed anything of who he was or why he ever wanted a son, daughter or wife who might want more than he could or ever wanted to give of himself. Money he threw in their faces to make up for the fathering he never wanted. Good son's goodness was to be part of this drama. It excited him beyond any encounter he had ever had with Barry or other boys or women who slipped in and out of insecure sheets of his dreams or the imaginings that sufficed to stem the tide of the swelling he endured from puberty through adolescence---from the urge to peel off his Speedo swimsuit during competitions while onlookers might stare in disbelief or applaud their approval to how he stood without shame or fear of consequence when naked on the bridge at Saint John's. Good son, star of the pool. All he had to do was score the best time and adulation would reign supreme. One's masculinity would never be questioned, even though a cruel God who never responded to prayers would leave the petitioner blanks to fill-in without the help of pontifical guidance or even the guidance of mere mortals who repressed the urge to smite one such as he with words cruel enough to kill.

Chapter 4

Vietnam

Male Iguanas: The main reason for not neutering the male iguana is that the results are so unpredictable.

Barry's dad looked so young the bartender at Minneapolis' Washington Bubba Bar refused to believe his 1948 I.D. "No beer for you, you little shit."

Sitting next to Rick was another inductee, who opened his wallet and furnished an I.D. The bartender didn't bother to check—he slid a Grain Belt tap beer down the bar.

"I'm old enough to get my ass shot in Vietnam, and I'm not old enough to suck a beer from your sorry-assed hand, for Chrissakes. My fucking I.D. Look. Twenty-two." Rick slapped his I.D. on the sticky bar. He picked up a napkin and shredded it.

"Listen, little beaver. I don't give a shit if your I.D. says you're President Johnson. You ain't gettin' no beer here."

"Hey. Don't sweat it," Daniel Cargill-Maximillian said as he patted Rick on the back He slapped a buck on the bar. "Yours," he nodded to the bartender. "I'll vouch for the little man." Daniel laughed. "We just finished our induction physicals. He wasn't so little standing there at the urinal with one hand pinching a cotton swab to stop the blood oozing from the prick who sliced his finger, and the other hand gripping his cock to squeeze a sample piss into the plastic cup. I think he needs some fluid."

The bartender swirled his bar rag above his head and touched his forehead in mock salute.

"We have a couple of hours before we leave. I don't think there'll be much beer at Fort Bragg for either of us. Give the little big man a break," Dan said. He slapped another buck on the bar.

Rick swiveled to his right, looked up and said, "You got that right, man." He offered his hand.

"Rick."

"Dan." He slapped Rick on the back.

The bartender nodded. "Inducted. I should've known. Drink up! And get out there and blow away some-ah those gook asses."

Daniel Cargill-Maximillian had never needed to claw his way to lofty places. He had failed enough tests and antagonized enough teachers to be bounced out of the prestigious upper Blake School in Minneapolis the first semester of his senior year. Family endowments to Saint John's University coffers as well as ACT scores in the thirties forced admissions counselors to admit him to SJU. He refused to be labeled a Cargill or a Maximillian. He worked hard to make the swim team in his senior year. Despondent from being cut from the swim team, he enlisted in the Army.

Dan and Rick flew from Lindbergh International to National Airport in Washington, D.C. They were bused to Fort Bragg, North Carolina with fifty sweating, farting, bitching Minnesota inductees for eight weeks of basic training. Having been awake for thirty-two hours, Dan and Rick encountered a drill sergeant whose lip not four inches from Dan's screamed, "Young blood. You are shit. And this is your shit hole. You and your shithole friend will—What the fuck is this? A book? You little pussy! You bring a book to my house? You think you'll have time to read a fucking book? Our enemy wants to blow off your nuts and you want to read a book? Answer me you little fucking piece of feces.

That's shit in your vocabulary. You little fuck." Ripping the cover from Daniel Cargill-Maximillian's paperback copy of Herman Hesse's *Narcissus and Goldmund,* he tore pages and shoved them into Dan's mouth. "Eat these words you little prick."

After enduring eight weeks of basic training, laughingly refusing to volunteer for Officers Training School, and surviving Advanced Infantry Training, Dan and Rick landed in Vietnam. Alternating walking point, they survived weeks of patrols. Their radio operator and only contact with command was a kick-ass Private First Class who called himself Mississippi Mudman from Baton Rouge. Dan teased him about coming from a city named after a red stick. Mudman laughed and said, "I love to rub my feet in the Mississippi mud and dream of the money I can make when I get back to my Mighty Miss."

He slipped his foot from his boots. "My feet white as yours. Is this jungle rot? We all gonna rot if we don't get killed first."

Second Lieutenant Bruckner ordered Rick, Dan and Mississippi Mudman to set trip flares far from the perimeter and to find cover. "Don't use the radio," Bruckner warned.

Dan, Rick and Mudman followed orders. M-16 rifles were as light as the toy guns Dan and Rick played with when they were kids. At breakfast mess they had talked about playing cowboys and Indians, always ganging up on the weakest or youngest kids to make them be the Indian victims. "Cowboys never died," Dan said. "I still have my Roy Rogers guns and holster." Rick said he and his buddies made wooden guns that shot thin strips of rubber tire inner tubes. They stung like hell and the kids who got shot yelped and fell to the ground. Mudman laughed. "God damn. Ain't no games I wanna play."

After setting up trip flares, they would normally return to the fire base, but Second Louie Bruckner had ordered them to take cover. Rick sucked in his breath and pumped up his chest.

He was ready to challenge the order. Dan put his hand on his shoulder and shook his head "No." So they hunkered down as low as they could. Blood swirls. Hearts thump. Black deep dark suffocates. Whump! Whump! RPG's. Trip flares explode. Claymores concuss. Grenades. Ears tick tap to M-16s. Trapped. Time telescopes. Alive? Breath on neck. Vomit. Motherfucker I'm alive. Somewhere there are the living. Cobra gunships unzip dark with tracers. Maggots feast on imaginations. Kick bodies into bush. Me. Me see maggots eating my body. Me see me inhale stench of their victory. My flesh stinking. Warm was my blood. Wipe. Smell. Taste. Salt. Breathe. Crawl fingers. Dig dirt. Ache. Arms fold me. Breath warms me. I am. "Rick," Dan whispers. Swabs spit from Rick's lip. Dan shivers. Rick shudders. Mudman huddles. Silence screeches silence of war's slop and stench. Explosion. Mudman jumps. Friendly or hostile fire no one ever knew. The world quiets. Mother Earth sighs.

Crawling, crouching and finally running they reached the firebase. Hunkered down. "Incoming" someone screamed. An explosive concussion knocked Rick to his back. In his limp hand a warm ooze stuck to Rick's fingers. Blindly searching for Mudman, he swallowed vomit. Childhood's memory of muscle drooping from his leg after he had run his bicycle's pad-less pedal through his calf makes him cry. He chokes.

Friendly flares burst, lighting up the perimeter. "Cut the dog tags, you stupid son of a bitch. Don't stand there like a pussy! Now!" Second lieutenant Bruckner commanded. A puff of air rose like a soul from the body bag he tossed at them. "Just cut off the goddamn dog tags and give 'em to me. Get the tags, you stupid son of a bitch."

"Motherfucker!" Rick raised his M-16. Between surges of pain and compassion his mind raced to find reason. Finding neither, Rick tossed the boot full of bone and blood, dog tag square-knotted in the bootlaces into the body bag. He waved his blood-smeared hands in the air. "Slurp! Sir! You killed him. You son-of-a-bitch. Your fucking orders killed him." Here, Rick thrust his hands at Bruckner's face. "Eat what's left of Mudman!"

"I will court martial your sorry ass, Corporal. Get the fuck out of my world," Buckner bellowed.

Rick and Dan returned to stand-down, a pause not as good as Rest and Relaxation with free government condoms and a flight to Hong Kong, but a time to sleep without fear.

"No need to worry about the second lieutenant's crap." Dan threw his arm over Rick's shoulder. "Fuck it, man," Rick said. "I'm gonna frag that mother fucker." Mississippi Mudman was one of the blackest and cover-your-ass buddies Rick had ever known. "Get the dog tags, you stupid son of a bitch. Now!" was all Rick would ever remember.

After days of restless sleep and patrols, after nights on stand-down when everyone in the platoon was too numb with beer and pot to think or dream, it was easy. Cathartic. No one had seen. On guard in night-black that brought a sapper attack, Rick tossed the grenade.

"Poor son of a bitch," Dan said as they slid the lieutenant's remains into the body bag. Rick cut Bruckner's dog tags from his boots. The zipper sang. "At least no one will have to look at his fragged remains in a coffin."

"Holy motherfucker! You are the man! Let's get some chow." Dan threw his arm over Rick's shoulder.

Rick shrugged Dan's arm from his shoulder. He turned his eyes into Dan's. "Look at me for Chrissakes. You wanna eat? We killed. We were there!"

Dan avoided Rick's stare. "Cut the shit. You. Not we. You are the hero. We gotta hoist a beer to honor of your guts—guts I never had."

"Fuck you, man. Just fuck you. Simple. Fuck you. Just shut the fuck up!"

Within a week of stand down from combat, all of the enlisted men knew the story of the fragging of the lieutenant. No one knew who.

Chapter 5
Señor Frogs

Iguana: Cold blooded iguana sleep. Warm
blooded humans steep.

Sun rises and sets over Bandaris Bay with a glow that invited tourists to fly with them as pelicans fly nest-ward like kites bedecked in vivid sunset pastels. Sun pierced Barry's dreams of hairless navels flat and round. A tan complemented his riot of black hair—shaded his dark eyes. Grasping his bladder erection with cupped hand, Barry subdued images of his mother and father's overwhelming sexual smoke. Between waking and dreaming, Barry fought to separate remembrance from reality, the they then them wafting, seeping upward through floor furnace-grate to his sense of unknowing. Sweet-perfume and man-smell curled upward to whet his dreams.

Barry replayed the scene over again while he sipped yet another margarita when he awoke after returning to #110. Afternoon became twilight so quickly he wasn't certain that what he had seen was real. Emily disappearing around the corner beyond Café de Olla. Mother racing after her. Tequila bottle empty, he reached for the mescal. Mescal Lajta. Cute little worm lazing at the bottle bottom appeared to want to be devoured. He poured the last ounce of mescal into his cup. Toyed with the worm. Punched at it with his forefinger. You're a tasty little critter I've been told. He swallowed the remains of tequila and worm.

35

Senor Frogs rocks into the late hours. Barry eyed the entrance. Couples were strobe in smoky light like cartoon figures from his youth. Barry squinted. Tried to clear his vision. *Rocas margarita will clear my vision,* he thought.

A male nubbin of a waiter slipped into a chair at Barry's right elbow.

"Amigo? May, I serve you?" He blew on Barry's cheek, his bristled chin whiskers brushing Barry's ear.

"No mas," Barry fingered the brown wrapping paper covering the table.

"You sign, *Amigo.* I sign Pedro on the paper. Lay a proper *propina* on the paper and you cannot imagine what this night might bring to you, Amigo." He eased his hand to Barry's shoulder. "Tonight two women come to find Pedro. You sign name of place. We meet. Pick one. We be two with one woman for half-price."

Barry, Max, Barry. Who would Barry be? He squeezed the magic marker between stiff fingers, tried to bend letters in his mind to extract words to spill on the table. From the smoldering ash of charred affairs, he scrawled:

Moans

smudge my rise

before my star 'rives

Barry lost his grip on the marker, dropped his head to the brown paper. A voice wormed through the mescal haze of his stupor. Get to bed now! Now! Voice roared. Raced him to bed. Folding pillow over face and ears "Yes" penetrated his want not to hear the voice. His "Goddamn. Goddamn." Her "Here. This. Kiss." His "Ahh yes." Ears could not stifle.

Raising his head from the table, Barry clumsily plucked a fifty peso note from his Minnesota Twins logo wallet, flicked it to the table where it landed to cover the "blot" of his scrawl. Boyz II Men's "I'll Make Love to You" echoed from a rafter of voices croaking something like song from the throats of Senor Frogs' bog of twenty, thirty and forty-something's. Barry wiped perspiration from his forehead, slicked back black hair with two hands, and swayed toward the exit. Bile rose. He swallowed. Coughed. Stumbled to the street where a cobblestone caught his foot. A sea breeze tossed his hair, soothed his senses, lured him to the beach.

Excited, Chase rode the elevator and walked through the open-air lobby toward the beach. His bare feet slipped on wet tiles. "Damn!" He looked left to the pool, right to the restaurant, directly ahead to the gate to the beach. Waves sounded, moonlit shadows urged him forward. Hurrying past the long-closed bar he skipped three steps to the gate. Locked.

He grasped the wrought-iron bars. Shook the gate. Trapped. He released his hands from the cool iron, fingered the white, rubber Tropicana wristband, felt an electric buzz flow from hands to shoulder to eyes. He pressed his hands over his eyes. Kellie a white shimmer and promise of peace stood at the altar. Chase locked his eyes with those of the Reverend. "I do." Here I am. Mr. She Mrs. She wife. I husband. Coupled by God. My God. Give me. Give me this happiness you promise as two-become-one.

Chase retreated to the steps to the left of the elevator. Raced two steps at a time to the hotel atrium, bounced up steps to the cobbled street. Reek of Tabasco and lime, fish and sewer gas seared his senses as he surged past black and broken garbage bags bulging beneath streetlights. Water from a broken sewage pipe spewed beneath his feet as he scrambled down the narrow passage to the beach next to Hotel Emperador. A dumpster loomed in front of him. He darted right, caught his toe on abroken cobblestone, righted himself, and gasped. Moonlit stars and surreal ships' lights blazed in Bandaris Bay.

He knew neither what he ran to or from. Nothing should have driven him from bed of his beautiful bride. Yet there was a longing—a longing he never understood. He had wrestled with reason and emotion through high school and college. Benedictine values had taught him to listen. Listen to heart and mind? Listen to Father and Mother? Conflict conquered his need to resolve his desires. He dug his toes in the sand. Moonlight obscured familiar stars. He folded his hands in prayer. "Father," he began.

"Chase?" A shadow stretched toward his shoulders. Warmth of a familiar voice made him unfold his hands to touch the hand on his shoulder. Not wanting to see, Chase closed his eyes, gently pushed the hand from his shoulder and held the voice at arms' length.

Awakened by explosions of crashing waves, Kellie bumped her head on the stucco wall. She ached for the smooth of Chase's lips. She gasped for air as she felt the cool of empty sheet. Heart pounding from confusion, she flipped the balcony light switch. Confusing light for shadow and shadow for light, her eyes raced to see where Chase might be. *A beach walk? Why? Why? Tension? Excitement?* Unable to sleep? She turned off the light. Eyes focusing slowly, she squinted to distinguish the sight of silhouettes on the beach. *Chase? No. Champagne? Of course. Champagne. They had talked of a champagne breakfast. But how would he bring the bubbly? Where chill it? Where buy it? No. Something's not right.* Seeking warmth from shudders rising within her, she wrapped her arms around her shoulders.

In faint moonlight she sensed Chase's shape. Shape dissolving from shadow. Male shadow. She knew male swagger as it disappeared into the distant black toward Blue Beaches Hotel. She had read of sailor's wives peering from their home's widow's walks as they peered to sea for their seamen's ship to return. The shadow she knew turned.

She fled to the bathroom, soothed her skin with Clinique lotion, spritzed her pubic hair with, with, with. In a panic that turned her sweet breath to gasps, Kellie searched in the spill of moonlight for her Essential Mist spray. No light. No more light, she panicked. She groped, fumbled fingers among the mess of crèmes, colognes, moisturizers, oils, emollients until her fingers clasped a solid rectangle. She sensed the nearness of Chase. Pressing the bottle to her cheek, the cool glass calmed her nerves. She pressed the atomizer with a delicate finger to freshen her privates. Scent of Polo assaulted her senses. No, no, no. Wrong. Caught in her flurrying fingers she groped for a washcloth. Hearing a slight movement at the door, she tiptoed from bathroom to bed.

Chase pinched the room key on the string round his neck. He stooped to the lock, inserted the key, worked it back and forth intentionally to create enough sound to awaken Kellie. His erection ached in the tight of his Speedo. Images. Chase grasped his penis, thrust it upward to expose it to the cool air beneath his navel. He listened for the squeak of the door hinge. No sound. He fought the urge to slip into the bathroom to relieve himself of his erection. Moonlight illuminated Kellie's naked arm and leg.

Kellie murmured. Slid her hand from above her head to slide the sheet to expose her naked hip. Chase peeled his Speedo over his erection with his thumbs. Slipped his suit over his buttocks. Peeled it to his ankles. Stepped naked. Eased to the bed. Wrapped a leg over Kellie's hip. Breathed on her cheek.

She, sensing without knowing, that this moment, this speck of time might draw him to or from her, rolled into his body's cup. Hands groped. He dived. Scent of Polo cologne surprised and inflamed him. Kellie pulled his head toward hers, but his strength was greater. He flipped like a diver coming out of a half twist and buried his lips in the sweet promise of Polo.

Chase tasted. Kellie ruffled his hair. He ached for more. She folded him to her. Chase began to explore a space he had never known. Kellie soared into dreams of this night eternal.

"Love me forever?" Chase whispered.

She dug her fingernails into his back until he squirmed with pain. "I have. I do. I will."

Chase bit his lip. Nails inflamed him. He felt a violent surge.

Kellie curled into a cocoon of self. Chase pressed closer to the fetal curl of her buttocks. Warmth. Satisfaction. Contentment. Happiness. Stay. He slid to the edge of the bed, slipped his feet to the floor. Crash of waves sprang him fully awake. Shuffling silently to the bathroom, he eased through the foggy glow of light. Nightstand clock's glow illuminated Kellie's cheek. Drawn to the roar of waves, the crush of the night's sexual explosion stunned him. He stood on the balcony. Two shadowed figures faced in the sand like a squatting Buddha.

Loving stabs, bleeds and leaves wounds no one sees. Some never heal. The beach is no place for the blues. Young hearts yearn for jazz, for jazziness without blues. Will jazz play the beach tonight? Finally, this night? Crash of waves wipes thoughts clean. Ocean's warp and weft of waves jam rhythms and pitches inviting souls to lose themselves in all that jazz.

Gleams of moonlight, crash of waves, remorse, and epithets spewing from his father's mouth congealed in Barry's knotting stomach. He didn't know whether to reach to the shadow or to withdraw to the place where all who sought to remake him in their images would harbor him. He kicked at the sand, felt it wet it his toes. He watched the approach. Thought he heard a saxophone moaning. Not jazz. Blues. Low. Way down low. Shaped like a child it approached.

Chapter **6**

Andales

Iguanas: Do not betray

Exhausted from running, fleeing, feeling abandoned by mother, father, brother, Emily curled in a fetal position near the artist who spewed grotesque images of demons with fiery tongues lapping at the breasts of cartoonish blondes from his toxic spray cans. Fumes overwhelmed her.

Jesus knelt. Waves splashed over the malecon misting him and Emily. Sculpted images, not quite human, not quite alien, climbed a ladder to the heavens. Emily lay crumpled like waste paper at his feet. *Police? Tourists? God? Brown skin? White skin?* Jesus knew not whether to abandon her to the stones, or to shield her with his arms. *She, they, are the ones who throw pesos to the wind like confetti—they who rise above malecon vendors and expectant waiters, they who soar above all things Mexican. July, August, September, October, November make us lie that rain will come. Sierra Madre wraps her arms around me. Holds me in an embrace from which there is no escape.*

Jesus wet his fingers on his lips to swab hers. Emily peered into the glistening pool of brown eyes. "You," she began.

Jesus put his fingers to his lips. "Sssh. Here." He slipped his hand under her arm.

Emily uncurled her legs, stood, leaned her shoulder into

41

warmth of Jesus' chest.

"Come," he said. "I will help you home."

"No, no. I cannot. I have no home. "

"Come. I have a place."

"No."

"You can wash hands. Face. And it's safe. Walk good. Feel better."

"No. Drink. I need a drink. Music. Music and a drink. Just one."

"We can go to Andales. Giant margaritas. But first. Some food here?" Jesus steadied her to a malecon stand serving roasted corn and soda.

Jesus dug deeply into his pocket for pesos to pay.

"Corn!" Emily said as she laughed. "Corn on a stick and dipped in butter. Let's sit."

The malecon's burst of lights strung around stalls offering strawberries and cream, caramel flans, cinnamon churros, apple enchiladas, and *tres leches* cake with berries among many other sweets invited everyone.

Emily pointed to the churros. *"Uno,"* she said. Looked into Jesus' eyes. Mother will never believe that I have captured our Jesus.

Emily and Jesus walked the malecon. Stood and soothed their faces with Pacific spray. They elbowed their way to the front of the local and international crowd watching the mime. Emily peeled her eyes as she tried to discern if there was a familiar face beneath the absurd whitewashed visage and the stovepipe hat.

"Take me away," she said

Jesus did not understand. He gently tugged at her arm. "Away?"

"There, just across the street. Music. Music and drink. I need them."

Car horns blared and tires screeched when Emily stepped

into the street. Jesus tried to pull her back to the sidewalk, but she demanded, "They will stop." And she pushed Jesus forward across the street where Master Baiters Fishing offered its ware and excursions. Emily giggled.

Bar Clairvoyance's open door and sidewalk-chalked sign offering Happy Hour margarita doubles for thirty pesos caught Emily's eye. Jesus followed her. Hours later Andales' tunes peeled Emily's inhibitions like skin from her sunburned shoulders. Music assaulted Emily's reason. She slid her pelvis into Jesus crotch. Together they throbbed. *Mary, Mother of Jesus, forgive me.* Jesus raised his eyes to the egg-cartoned ceiling. Emily ground her groin to his. Sweating with expectation, she swirled the ice in her grande margarita. She fingered and tossed cubes to the floor. "*Uno mas!*" She raised her glass high above Jesus' sweat-soaked forehead. A whistle assaulted her senses. She was blind. Hands gentled her head backward. A soothing voice urged her to open her mouth. Liquid fire exploded in her throat. Whistle shrieked. Hands shook her head. Sparks exploded into a spectacular kaleidoscope of colors.

Feeling arms holding her upright, faces surfaced. Images of the day quick-silvered in her mind like those in a fun house mirror. From Café de Olla where she had fled, a sweep of black hair delivering a tray. Yes, she had seen that before, this very day, somewhere early, before the escape from her mother, or was it last night, at the restaurant? Or was it in the past, the past further back than memory could recall. Black, brown, black, brown. Her mind's images strobed the light of her unknowing.

"You brought me here?

"Yes."

"Why you? You and your brown arms and face?"

"Come. Let's dance."

"Buy me a margarita? The fishbowl with rocks."

Jesus knew she should have no more.

Torsos swayed. Margarita glasses hoisted. Hips gyrating. Foreheads flopped on breasts to the rhythm of Chubby Checker's "Twist." "How low can you go?" a slurred voice buzzed Jesus' ear.

"I am high and low. I am whatever the night asks of me," a voice intruded.

Jesus and Emily nearly succumbed to music and sweat of the muscular arm embracing them.

"Amigo." Jesus cupped his hand on the bicep reaching through the scream of music and dervish of pelvic gyrations toward Emily. "I am paid to deliver this *senorita* to her *Madre.*"

"Hey! *Amigo.* No problem. Good job you have. Too young. Way too young for me. Too drunk. Way too drunk for me. Take her away." Biceps raised his arms high to Y as The Village People's "YMCA" screamed and rocked.

The vision of gnarled armpit hair, the stench of onion sweat oozing from biceps assaulted Jesus' senses. "Please?" he whispered to Emily. "I know a place. I will take you there. No more margaritas."

Emily folded into his arms, pressed her leg between his. "Take me," she gulped. "Take, take," she slurred. "Take me. One more mar-hard-rita before you take me?" A long sigh followed her words. No one had ever harmed her. "Hum, for wee, ahh, gome," she gulped, reached her hand to steady herself at a high table cemented to the floor, grasped a fishbowl margarita left by a dancer who still enjoyed energy and equilibrium and drank the dregs.

Jesus seized Emily's arm. Closed her to his chest. *"No mas. No mas."* He struggled to wrest Emily's limp torso through the sweltering Andale mob. He looked to the ceiling for help. Inverted egg-case dividers serving as cheap acoustical tiles blocked his appeal to the heavens. A stringy-haired, forty-something red head lifted her dress as she leaped to her perch on a table-stool cemented to the floor. A black vee fringe of fabric shimmied with her breasts as she jiggled and jumped, legs and arms flailing to the lyrics of "YMCA."

Jesus cradled Emily in his arms. "Pee," she slurped into his ear. "Gotta pee." He pushed aside a tattooed, forty-something male whose armpit dripped sweat from his purple tank top. Jesus slid his hand through a slot of space between the gyrating *gringo* and his wisp-of–bones partner, each balancing a glass of muddy liquid in a free hand while groping the other's buttocks. Jesus squeezed Emily between them to the *bano* door.

Emily flinched as the stumbled. Stars exploded. Beautiful. She shook her head. Ran her forefinger across her teeth. No gums? Raising her eyes to the mirror she steadied her stance with one hand on the sink. She weaved. Swooned. Green ants marched in military precision around the mirror's edge. Amazed, she reached to interrupt the rigidity of their lines. She twirled her head around and around while ants marched around and around beneath an exploding sky.

"Hey? Hey? Are you okay?"

Emily reached to touch the green ants scurrying to carry tiny loaves of white around the perimeter of the mirror. Babies. Bundles of babies. Each bowed to her. Offered her a baby before moving on. A thing with wings erupted. Emily slapped her hand to squash the thing with wings on the metal mirror that would not shatter. "Slut! You are the Queen!"

Jesus slid onto a vacant bar stool nearest the women's *bano*. His groin ached. Emily was close to his reaching. This promise. This she. Near touching. But how to steal her from here to *Velas Vallarta*, creating no scene? Slipping away between bars of music and shouts of "Alice? Alice? Who the fuck is Alice?" congealed in his mind. She. He. He had keys to vacant rooms. Keys to queen beds. Keys to refrigerator bars. For a few pesos Jesus had greased palms of maids. Winked at them for future favors. They grinned— knew he would tip them. This night would be his turn to fold back the covers of a queen bed at *Velas Vallarta*. Undiscovered by everyone but Juanita, he, Jesus, would know ecstasy.

Emily vomited. Spewed the mirror.

"You gross little bitch," a deep-throated voice called to her from her wilderness.

She wiped her mouth with brown paper hanging from the dispenser next to her shoulder. "I, I, am not a bitch. No. Am not. I am with Jesus!"

"Hey, little lady. I'm not Jesus. Maybe you should pray, but I can help you while he waits." A deep-throat voice soothed as its hands massaged Emily's back. "None of us is ever what we seem to be. Come." The voice attached itself to a hand that gentled Emily toward the door.

"Do you smoke?" a beige-complexioned, twenty-something male disguised in a purple-striped, knitted hat asked Jesus.

"Sometimes," Jesus said.

Linked like marionettes dancing to a samba, the deep-voiced drag queen elbowed Emily through the swirling crowd. "This yours?" he winked at Jesus. "Not my flavor, but she is cute. And drunk as hell. Says she's with Jesus. Jesus!"

Jesus shoved aside the hand offering the joint in his rush to gather Emily.

"Fifty pesos for one," the knit-hatted kid shouted above the roar of "Alice? Alice? Who the fuck is Alice?" into Jesus' ear.

"Alice. Who the fuck is Alice?" the Andale crowd's voices reverberated.

The drag queen reached into his bra. Retrieved pesos for two joints. He tucked them into Jesus' shirt pocket and uttered in his sexiest voice, "Do me later little brown man after you savor her."

Lost in the din of voices, Jesus swaddled Emily's hands in his. Her eyes drooped. He braced his hip to hers, thrust his leg between to create a tripod.

Andale's: is a historical icon in Puerto Vallarta . . . opened twenty-five years ago by Jorge and he still runs the place (with the help of his son Jorge Jr.) Famous for wonderful and great times. You're guaranteed to recognize the music . . ."Who the F--- is Alice" (she tied to the staircase) and "The Pussy Song (meow), just to name a few (quite the eclectic variety of music here, along with the clientelle). Andale's patrons return night after night and year after year . . . you'll always see the same hunters there! Andale's: Internet post

Mornings, he delivered room service at Hotel Tropicana. Afternoons, Jesus managed maids on the fourteenth floor of the west tower of *Velas Vallarta*. Evenings he waited tables at Coco Tropical. Sleeping a few hours before dawn, he dreamed of blondes and Juanita. If only the Virgin Mary had been blonde, he, Jesus would have never gotten off his knees. But here, with his leg planted between Emily's feet amid the screaming call and response of Wreclox-N-Effect's "All I wanna do is zoom-a-zoom-zoom-zoom and a poom-poom. Just Shake Ya Rump" rising toward the egg-carton ceiling, Jesus knelt to cup Emily's face in his hands.

Jesus learned from Juanita how to respect and romance a woman. Having charmed the thirty-something maid with a smile and a delicate brush of hip to hip, he curved his arm around her as they watched the sun effervesce into the Bay of Bandaris. She extracted a master key from her white apron while warning that the Jacuzzi needed repair.

Embracing each tile with the sure-footed matador's strut,

Jesus walked Emily to the employee entrance to *Velas Vallarta*.
The cool of Emily's arm warmed his fingertips as he guided
her steps.

"Ah, um," she murmured. "I," she looked up into his face.
"I am so . . ." she began as she stumbled over the barrier of her
mind that had always protected her from harm.

Stepping into the elevator, Jesus, knowing there was no
thirteen, punched lighted cube fourteen. Its pastel glow soothed
him. Emily leaned against him, wound fingers with his. He
tugged at her hair.

"Hurts," Emily murmured.

"Sorry." Afraid that hurt would overwhelm her, he felt
hurt exploding. Juanita? He and she dreamed of golden futures
beginning with each *Puerto Vallarta* sunrise. Juanita? Can three
become one?

The elevator door opened with a rush of air. Emily swooned.
Jesus scooped her into his arms. Carried her to 1414 *Velas
Vallarta*. Softening her cheek to his, she clung.

"Don't let the green queen ants eat my face."

"No. No green ants. No." Jesus gently spilled her to the
king bed, lifted her head with this right hand, cupped his left
to suppress his erection. Conditioned air caressed his sweating
forehead. He covered his heart to silence the throbbing. He knew
someone was watching. Mother? Mary? Juanita? Want this fire.
Will be damned. He smoothed Emily's hair with light fingers.
Lay his hand on her breast.

"Holy Mother Mary of God forgive me," he exhaled as he lay
beside her. Her upper lip thinned. His swelled. His blonde angel
from el Norte was nothing more than a pale shadow of a dream that
he could not will to be real. He gentled his hand beneath her head.
Lips close to hers, he sensed no breath. Calm. He knew he needed
calm. He patted her face. Emily moaned. Opened her eyes.

"Sleep," she murmured.

"We will," Jesus whispered, his lips nibbling her ear. "Here. Sit up." He eased from her side of the bed. Reached for matches in the ashtray. Finding the book of Velas Villarta matches, he sat up.

"Sleep," Emily breathed. "Tropical."

"Will. We will," Jesus said. He slipped one of the joints from his shirt pocket. Struck a match. Lit. Inhaled. Coughed. "Will sleep." He blew smoke into her ear and cat-lapped her lobe.

Emily buried her head in her pillow. "No," she sobbed.

Jesus' head thudded to the sheet. Anger swelled. Tease. Another tease from *el Norte*. She will not do this to me. Juanita chastised. He wobbled erect. Stabbing the joint with a vengeance rarely seen in the bullring, he threw the remains at Emily. Reeling from want of sex, he slammed the door and leapt into a pool of darkness.

Emily fought herself awake. The ache of her forearm crooked beneath her brow drew her senses to the surface of consciousness. The cold crisp of sheet startled her. Blurry. Tongue thick. Sharp breath. Gasping. Emily tugged at the bedside lamp's chain. Light seared Emily's eyes. Her conscious mind screamed, "Alone." She unwound herself from the tangle of sheet, punched O on the phone. An annoying length of rings made her heart race.

"Hola?"

"Do you speak English?"

"Si."

"Si? Yes?"

"Ring me a taxi, please."

"Si."

Stumbling to the door, she slid into the elevator, punched the lighted lobby cube. She leaned her forehead against the wall's cool. Where do I go? What do I do? Jesus? The ding of the elevator's bell and bumpy stop startled her. She lifted her body from the wall and sank into the opening. A taxi waited.

"Hotel Tropicana *por favor*," she said.

"*Si.*"

Nearing Amapas Calle Emily recognized scenes from her morning walk. "Stop." Purse open, she fingered and offered a two hundred-peso note. "Air! Need air," she gasped. Smoothed her hair with a sweaty finger as she careened down Pulpito. Stench of raw fish and sewer gas made her retch. She covered her mouth, stepped through the gush of water from a broken pipe. When she reached the sand, she stepped out of her sandals, reached to retrieve them and tucked them in her handbag. She turned left to walk along the beach to the Hotel Tropicana where she dreaded she would have yet another confrontation with Mother. The sound of crashing waves obliterated her thoughts. Green ants invaded her thoughts, marched on the edge of her mind's mirror. Hundreds of ants. She was amazed at the rigidity of their lines as they marched round and round her reflection, creating a pulsating halo. She squinted. Shook her head. Tried to shake the image from her mind by twisting her head from side to side.

Chapter 7
Blizzard

Iguana: Survive in exotic locations

January, after separation from service the previous summer at Fort Ord, Rick hired a cab to drive him from the Minneapolis Lindberg International Airport after his short flight from Rochester. They had been delayed upon departure while the plane was de-iced. Rick leaned his head against the cab's cushioned backseat while the Cabbie chattered as they drove west through snow and wind toward Wayzata. Dan had asked Rick to be his best man. Rick regretfully accepted.

"No shit little beaver. You are the best of all men!" Dan's voice rang across the miles when he phoned.

"Fort Snelling National Cemetery is just over there on the right. Can't see much with the snow and dark. But it's there. Filled with remains of heroes. Wives too. Heroes and heroes' wives. Those hippie kids who splashed blood downtown on the induction center steps should be shot. Bunch of American assholes wearing the footprint of the chicken 'round their necks as a peace symbol. You must ah wanted them hung by their scrawny necks," the Cabbie rattled. "Nam vets? All our war vets are buried there."

Rick slunk farther into the cab's cool leather.

"You say Nam?"

"Yah."

"Jesus H. Christ. Jesus. Be goddamned proud. That's what you gotta be. Proud. Don't care what nobody says. We shouldah wasted 'em all. Cleaned up the planet. How many gooks didya kill?"

"Fuck you!"

"Whoa. I didn't mean Nothin'."

"You ever looked at all those crosses?"

"Hell yes. Every day."

"You know they have names?"

"No shit?" He twisted his head to look at Rick. Sneered.

"Look at the fucken' road, man. You wanna kill me?"

"Why would I do that? Don't even know your name."

Rick spat on the cab's floor.

"It's so fucking cold. Turn up the heat."

"You don't like it?" the Cabbie joked as he looked for the face in the rear view mirror.

"Lived here nearly all of my life. Still hate it."

"Son of a bitchin' snow. All this goddamned wind and snow. I don't usually drive anybody anywhere in this shit. We can pull off. Fucking semis, pardon my French, blow snow so we can't see shit. Ah shit. Here blows another one. Hang on. Can't see a fucking thing."

Rick closed his eyes. Leaned back on the seat and swallowed the bile creeping from throat to mouth. *Ain't gonna die here.* "Screw it," he said. "Just drop me anywhere you can find an exit near a motel."

Two semis passed and spewed blinding snow. Cabbie struggled to right the car as it swayed like a horny whale and beached itself in a three-foot drift of snow.

"No further," the Cabbie said. "No shovel. No boots. No nothing but sit." He called the dispatcher. Told her he and his fare were stuck somewhere on 494 between the airport and the curve north toward I-494. "Wayzata. Yes. The fare is headed for Wayzata. For a wedding. In January. In Minnesota. Yah. Right," the Cabbie laughed.

Rick couldn't make out much of the garbled response from the dispatcher. His thoughts locked. Why had he agreed to be Dan's best man? He leaned forward, clasped his hand on the back of the passenger seat. "What's so fucking funny?"

"Sorry, but . . ." the Cabbie began.

"No sorry, man. It's your sorry ass that got us stuck here, and I ain't in no mood to spend a few hours in the back of your fuckin,' reekin' cab. So tell me what's so fuckin' funny."

Dan had telephoned Rick to tell him they would meet at Dan's father's house in Wayzata where the stag party would begin. From there they would drink by limo to Solid Gold where they would finger bucks into the g-strings of lovely twenty-something babes. For an ironic twist they would consummate the stag at the Gay Nineties.

Dan called Candace to inform her that the bridal party should not leave her apartment even though his father had arranged for the White Carriage Limousine to transport them to any destination they chose for any number of hours they requested. The forecast of snow, blow, and cold was much too dangerous for the girls to venture out. Candace agreed. Dan was worried that Rick would be stranded at the airport. Without his best man in tow at the stag party, it would be a bust. He wanted to see Rick's face when lap dancers teased his groin. He slipped into his L L. Bean jacket. Zipping quickly he swallowed the last drops of Drambuie. Warmth swelled from throat to stomach.

Dan backed his 1966 Mustang into six inches of new fallen snow. *Why the hell didn't I give him a phone number?* "Dammit." He jammed the gas pedal to the floor. Tires spun. He slammed the gearshift to neutral, eased up on the gas pedal. Thrust the gearshift into second. Mustang inched forward. Right arm over the seat, neck craned, squinting his eyes as if he had suddenly emerged from darkness to brilliant light he reversed, and hunched his shoulders as he peered through the falling snow. He backed down the driveway and maneuvered down Cargill Lane to the highway. His back ached from the tension of hunching forward to make some sense of all of the white falling. Surrounding. Obscuring. Cushioning. Entombing him. He knew there was a gentle curve where the road bent east toward Bloomington and the airport. But it had disappeared in the blindness the storm brought.

The sound of the Mustang's front bumper buffeting snowdrifts was like a fist pounded into a pillow. Dan grew more and more determined to meet Rick at the airport as he broke through each drift of snow. Snow spray engulfed the Mustang's headlights as it burst on the windshield with an audible hush that blinded Dan. If he slowed to ten miles per hour, he would get stuck in the snow. If he pushed forward faster, he could rear-end a car, a truck, anything stuck in the sea of blindness ahead of him.

The Mustang's rear skid left. Dan cranked the steering wheel right. Jammed the accelerator. The Mustang's rear swung violently to the left. Dan's muscles blazed with the fire of scotch-in-the-throat as he gripped the steering wheel. He tried to choke the Mustang into submission. Slammed the four-speed shift into reverse. He thrust his head, shoulders, back into the seat while slamming rigid feet into clutch and brake. All his weight, force and will did not right the Mustang. He battled his blood for hearing. *Where the hell am I? And where do I go when I don't know where I am? Freeze. I will slide into a storm and freeze. Dad will call. I know he knows where I am going. He will send the snowplows.*

Rick leaned over the front seat, tapped the Cabbie on the

shoulder and growled, "I'm gonna sue your ass, your cab company's ass if one little hair on my ass is harmed. You read that loud and clear?"

"Hey, man. Relax. I don't know where you come from. But this is Minnesota. We are survivors. We got gas in the tank and brains in the bank. Relax."

"No fuckin' way am I gonna relax, asshole." Rick pushed the door against the foot of snow, surprised at how much strength it took. "I see lights. I ain't sitting here sweating with you." He stepped into the snow—looked to the glow of light that was nearly obliterated by the tacit symphonic fall of snow.

Rick stepped from the cab. Mind reeling. Rick would throw another grenade and blow this cab. *Action. I can kick ass of any fool who crosses me.* "Get your ass in charge," his conscience throbbed.

"Don't think you can just walk out of here," the Cabbie warned. "Meter says you owe twelve bucks."

"No shit little beaver, as if you've ever smelled one. Tuck this Lincoln up you ass and call the fucking cops." Rick rumpled the bill and threw it into the cab. He reached back to shove the door closed. Falling snow flecked freeway lights, penetrating the dark.

"Goddamit," Rick swore to the biting wind. "Get me the fuck out of here." His Converse tennis shoes did not warm his trudge through the snow. *"Tomorrow,"* he thought. *"Tomorrow I will be gone. Fuck this. Fuck Dan. Fuck this . . . ."* He stumbled and fell full face into the snow. Snow swabbing nose, eyes and mouth, he struggled to wade through mounds. Purple light blinked VACANCY across the freeway's cascading curtain of snow. *Suitcase?* He panicked. *No clothes. Underwear. Need. Need to be clean. Too much dirt in the past. Better to be clean and vacant.* The eerie siren song of wind summoned him.

Dad? For Chrissakes! Why did you ever bring me to

Hayfield? Mother? You should have stopped him. Grandfather offered you and him a place to live. Live. Goddamit, I will live. And I have come back. Never. Never should have thought of this as home. Light snow, fluffy, the kind that made one sing "Let it snow and lie down in warmth" while one sipped brandy beside a wood burning stove and all of the animals were in the barn swept his mind free of debris.

Hayfield. Rick knew he was condemned to return there, to survive there. He thought he had escaped the farm after he and Dan had separated from Vietnam. But the black WAC who had separated from service with him at Fort Ord, she who had promised warmth beyond the gate, she had fled east.

As a teenager he could wade through two and three-foot drifts of snow so light it felt like feathers sifting from the sky. But he remembered how quickly a wind would roar out of the sweetness of a gentle snow, blowing up a blizzard.

Rick stumbled, eyes stinging with snow. Blinked. Childhood stuck to his tongue. Stung. Aching to lie down in the snowy mattress, his forehead collided with metal. He collapsed into a comforting cushion of snow.

Jerked into consciousness by the sound of the bump against metal, she who would become his Rose of Sharon, slid across the seat, wiped her breath's condensation from the passenger window, peered into the swirling snow. Paranoia. Sounds unreal. She looked to the gas gauge. Dark. She pulled on the dashboard switch. Light. Battery still alive. Why hadn't she listened to the warning? Warning to stay off the roads. She felt reassured for having filled the tank before she left work at J. C. Penney's in Southdale. Stalled just a few blocks after the turn off France Avenue, she wished she had listened to Dawn. She had warned that the storm could turn into a blizzard.

"Don't try to get home," Dawn had begged. "Didn't you see

the warnings on television? No travel advised in the greater Twin Cities area tonight. That's bad."

"I know, but they always exaggerate. Cry wolf so the sheep stay safe. I hate that. And all they want to do is boost their ratings. You know, it's only a few miles' drive up I-494 and a few blocks more to my apartment," she argued. "And we aren't living in Siberia, for God's sake," she laughed. "No one freezes to death nowadays."

"Well, babe, I'm staying here." Dawn begged Sharon to return the pledge.

"Can't," Sharon said. "I love you, but Richie needs to be let out. Can't let him soil my new carpet," she laughed.

A faint tap sounding like ice pellets ticked at her window. Illuminated by purple flashes of light a face fell against her window. *Out of heaven drop angels and demons,* she thought. She had read Milton's description of the fall. She was smart enough to rarely mention Milton to men she encountered in metro bars. Liberally educated at the College of Saint Benedict, she often felt shunned by coworkers who could not understand why she hadn't landed a better job and a sexy man. A puckered octopus-gray face slid sideways down the window. Angel or demon? She had taken to heart the Benedictine value of welcoming others both as individuals and as a community after her four years of liberal Catholic education. Look. Listen. Welcome.

The face slid down the glass. She cranked the window, reached her left arm and snared a mass of wet hair. It melted away like spring snow. Pulling hard on the door handle, she pushed against the door with her shoulder. Gusts of snow-driven wind stung her cheeks. Pellets pierced her cheeks. Couldn't open her eyes. Yet she pushed one hundred and twenty pounds of fragile weight against the door. Hopeless. Helpless. Blizzard. Blizzard's face—blocking the door. "Never leave your vehicle in a severe snowstorm," the weathermen always warned.

Sharon's coat belt snagged on the gearshift between the bucket seats. She tried to slide to the passenger seat. Reaching with her right hand, she pulled frantically until she heard her coat's belt rip. She pulled on the passenger door handle. Shouldered all of her weight against the door. Spears of electric pain shot from shoulder to brain. Desperate to know if the face was a figment, she opened the window and slithered into the bed of snow's biting wind. Nearly blinded, she reached for the door handle. Missed. Fell forward. Head crashed against metal. Conscious. Frantic. She stretched her arm to find the edge of the open window. Fingers throbbed. Burned. *Gloves. Where? Why no gloves?*

Stumbling with numbed hands from window to passenger-side mirror. She fumbled for metal. Beside the snow-covered fender she lifted leg after weary leg. She felt around. *Headlight?* Numb fingers sent bizarre messages to her brain. *Warm. Get warm. Good to be warm. To sleep. Lie down. This bed is soft.* She fell to her knees into cupped hands that pulled her from the door.

Rick willed himself mortal. Pushing her aside he wrestled the car door and pinned it open against the drifted snow. He, knowing there was no escape from wind, snow and cold, smoothed his fingers across her forehead, melting her eyebrows with his touch. Drill sergeant had hammered into his consciousness that two would not freeze if they pressed flesh to flesh; tucked hands between armpits, cocooned warm thighs to draw blood to each body's core. Drill sergeant never talked of warming of souls. But he did talk of nuclear attack. "Run to the nearest fox hole. Pull your rain poncho over your head and don't look at the blast."

Rick tugged, pushed, shoved until the bulk of human flesh rose up. He prayed for nuclear warmth. How could this body numb so fast? With all of his strength he crawled across legs folded in snow. *Tiny legs. Woman? I can carry this.* He wrested her through the open car door.

"Dammit!" He slapped the bundle of coat. "Wake up. Sit up. For Chrissake."

Arms attached to the body stirred. Sharon pushed. Rick unzipped his coat, pulled her toward him, ripped buttons from his shirt, snaked her hands into his armpits. She stirred. Warmth. Minutes of warmth meant survival. Minutes might become hours. Plows would come. Two bodies entangled in survival skins could make one.

Dan sensed the futility of rocking the Mustang forward and backward. Nowhere to go. He smelled rubber on ice as he rocked, neither moving forward nor backward. There was no escape from hot ice beneath tire ruts. He prayed that Candace had the sense to have her bachelorette party at her apartment as he had suggested. *Fuel gauge empty. Damn. Where am I? Rick? Us?* Not wasted this way. He switched-off the ignition, set the emergency brake. How peaceful and silent it would be to lie back in the seat to dream of wedding his beautiful Candy—having the most beautiful blonde in his arms and his best friend at his side as they stood at the altar while guests waited to sip Doris Duke's gift of Dom Perignon.

Snow swirled, piled, drifted, swathed the land in white drifts that shrouded abandoned autos in albino blimps. Dan burned with the need to find Rick. Rick. *Rick at the airport. I promised to meet him. Never broke a promise to him in Vietnam.*

Fear blazed in Rick's eyes when both knew what he had done. Scorch of flesh, stench of ash infused Rick and Dan with the reek of death. They had huddled together in the swill of the night as sappers surged past them. "It's over. Wasted," Rick breathed into Dan's ear. "No," Dan squeezed his hand around Rick's wrist. "Sssh. Listen." Their breaths were close, hot. "Gone. Sappers gone." Dan shuddered, his whisper flailing loosely in his mouth.

Dan relaxed his grip on Rick's arm, felt the electricity drain from his hand to his heart. He dared to breathe once more. But he could not catch his breath. On fire. He felt on fire. The electricity of Rick's arms burned. Mudman threw his arms around them as the huddled together.

Chapter 8
Romantic Zone

Iguana: in captivity may need care for more than twenty years

Candace nestled knees to bosom. Emily's face faded in the quiet, dreamy mist whispering she will return. She always has. Dreaming before Dan, Chase, Emily crept into her dream of a past life—the ache of frenzied groping in the heat of nights after football games enflamed her. Her heat made boys shiver from want. Heat of Vietnam she would never know. Whenever she uttered Vietnam, Dan turned cold. This night her dream chilled: Emily wresting from her grasp—running. Emily, forever running through a kaleidoscope of runs and returns. Dream unedited. Images fast forwarding, dissolving into swirling mists of unknowing.

Reporters swirled around her. Microphones drooped from clouds. "Your daughter. She is missing since how long?"

Candace swept manicured nails through wisps of sea-scented hair. "Emily, my sweet Emily." *Make tears. Flutter eyelids. Slip back upon heels.* "She had such beautiful hair. Blonde." She fluffed hers with both hands. Shook her head. "Has. Has beautiful blonde hair," she gasped and lowered her head to wipe tears that would not come. She paused to wipe a wisp of hair from her forehead. *Blink. Blink rapidly. Exhale. Camera get this.*

"Please tell   us what you know of your daughter's disappearance."

"Somebody has her. Emily would never. Has never." Candace paused, flutter her eyelids, covered her mouth. Gasped. Blinked directly into the camera and said, "Has never. Never run off. Never." She implored the camera. "Whoever you are, I beg you. Bring my baby, my baby Emily, back," she gasped and covered her mouth. Peered into the camera, "Back to me."

Spying the CNN logo on the cameraman's hat, Candace dived into his eyes. *What could be better? This is so much better than the tiresome cocktail parties with those second-marriage, trophy wives in Wayzata who had honed and toned their bodies with a ferocity unknown to the television workout mavens of the world.*

Candace exercised them on her Wayzata home-pool deck. After she dismissed the six few-fit and two far-too-fat would-be belles again, Candace slipped out of her bikini and into the naked water. She knew the recently hired pool boy would soon arrive to swab the deck. She enjoyed jesting with pool boys to see just how intuitive they might be. She would ask them if they brought filters, a metaphor for condoms in her mind. Her faux-tan reflected sprinkles of sun. She cupped her eyes to shield from the sun's heat while she floated on her back.

The pool boy, with a golden tan and abs well toned appeared as if he were a fallen Icarus. She snared the boy's eye, held it until he began to swell before her eyes. He came to her.

"Barry. Come a little closer. Here. On the edge of the pool."

"Yes Mam," Barry gulped as Candace wet her lips with her middle finger.

Radiating a smile to melt his chocolate eyes, running the stunning blue of her eyes deliberately from his forehead to his toes, she offered her hand. "Please. Please help me from the pool.

I am not a Mam." She crooked and wiggled her pointer finger at him as she summoned him and the swell his cupped hands feebly attempted to cover. "Please help me from the pool. Come. Did you bring the filters?" Candace giggled. "If not, you'll have to settle for your eyes on a skinny dip today."

He cupped his hands to cover his bulging Speedo. "I, I didn't know I was supposed to," he stammered. "To bring filters." *Chase's mother. Christ! Filters! She thinks I'm really stupid.*

He is more than twenty and much less than thirty for Chrissakes Candace thought as she turned her nude backside to him. *Chase's age.* "Come." She waved her hand over her shoulder. "Don't be shy!" She was grateful that she had hired him immediately upon the first interview. No references needed. He was needed. With a hip twist and a pout of lips she swirled to him, pressed nipples into his, curled her tongue to the tip of his lip.

He stumbled. Fell heavily onto the concrete, his mind and erection aching. *Chase's mother?*

I win. Again. Again a winner. Older. Wiser. Sexier. Alive in lust. I win, Candace thought. "Go now. Bring the filters next time!" She spread the towel on the chaise. Lay naked on her stomach.

Candace's dream burst and she bolted upright. Perspiring. Thirsty. Used to being pampered day or night, she rang room service. Bar closed. Kitchen closed. Pool closed. Why had she booked this hotel? Advertised as "Romantic Zone." Never had she stayed in a place with so few amenities. Tile and white paint everywhere. Romance? Gazing at the sunset as brown pelicans flew in formation toward the Sierra Madre—romantic? Cocktails served from trays held high above Rio de Janeiro's hunky waiters' hip-swings, that was romantic? Twisting one's neck to carve out a memory of the scene might be good for acrobatic lovers, but not for Candace. Aruba. She had written the check for Chase and

Kellie's honeymoon. They, soaking up Aruba's sun and enjoying five-star accommodations while she lay here sweating.

Candace had tried to convince Emily without cajoling that it was Daddy's suggestion that the five star *Velas Vallarta* was the best place to stay for rest and relaxation after the wedding. The Romantic Zone offered fine restaurants and civilized clientele and there Emily might find the man of her dreams. "We can taxi from *Velas Vallarta* to the Romantic Zone, sweetheart," Candace had implored. Emily spread her legs in the autumn swirl of Wayzata's scurrying leaves, crossed her arms, lifted her nose high enough to collect rain. She stared into the heavens for relief from the grief of having to mourn for a mother who just did not understand real romance. "Mother! I need the Romantic Zone." *Too smart,* Candace thought. *Always too smart for her age. Always reaching.*

Candace squinted at her Tropicana room's moonlit walls. *Emily,* she thought, *for God's sake, why don't you phone me? A little tiff, a minor squabble, too many times, too many years to be taken seriously. Smart. Emily. Always too smart and too knowing for her age. She and Amanda, always too smart. Phone Dan? No, it will be his same controlled response over and over again.* Candace tiptoed to the balcony. *For God's sake,* she thought. *A person can't even sit if she wants to view the beach and ocean at the same time.* A three-foot high concrete railing blocked her view. A gecko scurried away when she reached her hand to inspect a shadow. She could stand or sit on top of the air conditioner projecting from the wall to the balcony if she wanted to see the beach. She stood.

Movement. Silhouettes. Male? Yes. Male. No male image ever escaped Candace's sight or imagining. One image slid from a shadowed *palapa* into moonlight. Four arms stretched shoulder to shoulder. One pushed the other away or drew the other nearer? She squinted. Blood flooded Candace's cheeks. She massaged her temples. She leaned over the balcony as two shadows became one. Her heart throbbed. Feeling fire she could not smother, she ached to see as the two parted.

Angry, lonely, lust-filled, wishing she could find and hold Emily in her arms, so she could slap her into adulthood, Candace threw her arms around herself. Blood-cold, she swirled from the balcony. Fled to bed. Wound herself into a dream where she could bend reality to her will.

Emily and thirteen-year-old friend Amanda Thorpe, daughter of the company's corporate lawyer Alexander Thorpe III, had planned yet another sleepover at Emily's house. Candace often wondered why Amanda never asked Emily to sleep over at the Thorpes. She was ever more curious when she read *The Minneapolis Tribune* Society page headline "Justice Thorpe Divorces." Text: "Justice Thorpe III who served on the Minnesota Supreme Court with the distinguished Minnesota Justice former Minnesota's Viking's Alan Page said his love for his wife has never wavered. Irreconcilable differences led both to part amicably. 'I immediately deeded our Wayzata property to her. All I asked is that our precious dog Athena remain with me.'"

Candace kicked a silk sheet from her leg, rolled to her side to check the time on the bedside's Tiffany clock: 2:00 a.m. Giggles? Was she hearing giggles? No. Giggles so far away. Far, far away. She blended giggles into her dream. Fitting selves into maroon and gold high school cheering sweaters, they giggled and hugged while junior cheerers stuffed bras with tissues. Candace shook herself awake. Grasped her breasts. Nightmare-free of high school football scorers grasping her crinkling breasts, she awoke. Shook herself away from the dream. Slipping from silk sheets she stole to the stairs. Tiptoed through one of three great-rooms to where a shaft of light streamed from beneath the kitchen door to the tile floor. Giggles.

"Freak. Freaking good," Emily giggled. Careful not to make a sound, Candace nudged her pounding heart to open the door. She gasped. Prayed Emily hadn't heard.

Light shrieked from stainless steel refrigerator doors. A half-gallon orange juice carton leaned precariously against a Ketel One vodka bottle. Amanda's head, amid a torrent of hair, spewed onto the counter. Emily tapped Amanda's head. "Aw, c'mon. Let's make another big screw, "she giggled. "Driver. Big screw. Big screwdriver." She dribbled drops of orange juice and vodka from her glass onto Amanda's hair.

"Mah, um, mahgar-eet-ahs. Daddy said not," Amanda burped. "Not to drink. Drink not. Ah. Those."

"God's sake! You. You. Your. Your father. Thank you God he isn't. Isn't here?" Candace seized Emily's glass. Smashed glass and screwdriver in the sink. "You little, you little Daddy's girl. You drinking!"

Emily tongued her lips. *Mother,* she thought. *You send Chase off to college. You cage me here. Free. Let me free.* Her heart and mind would not abandon her.

"You, you with your parade of pool boys serving cocktails. I saw." Emily twisted her hands. "You. Fuss. Fuss over Chase. Never me!" Emily whirled. Candace grabbed Emily's wrist, dug her manicured nails in so hard she drew blood. Emily wrenched from Candace's grasp. Stumbled to the kitchen door. Sheer-white curtains caught blood from her wrist as she fled.

Emily fled, trusting her spirit to carry her close to destruction, and yet rescue her from the precipice of annihilation. She feared no harm. Armed with enough spunk to deliver a blow to those who tried to control her, she knew how to outwit lady iguana as well as the male of any species.

Exhausted beyond sleep or reason, Candace sank into the

breakfast nook's bench. Struggling to control the beating she always took when Emily escaped, Candace imagined a stage. There she choreographed every move. There she plotted every rising and falling action—every climax. Behind her mind's curtain, shapes grew in her imagining. Emerging from shadows, four arms muscled her to the sand. One's lips met hers. Another's tongue inched crab-like, flicked open her peignoir at its cleavage. Eyes wide open, she summoned moonlight to fill her from crown to toe with ecstasy. Lady Macbeth be damned. Candace was not cruel. No Lady Macbeth she. With each blink of eye her heart fluttered. Lip-like fingers probed, slid into a mouth aching to be explored. She arched her back on the nook's cushion. Rising, she stumbled to the washroom left of the kitchen door where Emily had fled. Pulling open the cherry wood medicine cabinet door, she reached for Doctor's pills. She cupped her hand around a water glass and slid the promise of sleep into her mouth. "Come home to Mommy Emily. I'm always here."

Minnesota moons cool summer skies. Winter's moons expose animals to prey. Snow elongates shadows. In Jalisco when the moon is full, iguanas close eyes to the light. In Minnesota when the moon is full, lovers light heat lamps in iguana terrariums. To succumb to the Puerto Vallarta warmth with no fear of frost or freezing, iguanas lay on branches near the flea market and on tiled roofs of places such as Playa los Arcos and in the canopy along Rio Caule. Tourists click photos of the exotic while native iguanas do not blink. It is in this misunderstanding that revelation may come to the warm blooded.

Chapter 9
Saint John's
Friday Night: Puerto Vallarta's waves rush to crush even the unwary iguana.

From Tropicana's balcony Kellie watched without knowing. Barry reached to embrace Chase. Chase's stiffened arms pushed him back while his fingers tensed to pull him toward him. Waves crashed, exploded in the quiet Mexican night.

"You can't be here!" Chase whispered.

"I didn't know." Barry's voice was childlike, lost in sweep and roar of a monstrous wave coursing to shore. "I didn't know. Didn't know. You? Here."

"I, I love. Love. Love Kellie. Love you."

Barry turned his back.

Chase eased gentle hands behind Barry's ears. Closed Barry's face in his hands. "God forgive me."

"No more," he whispered as he eased Chase's hands from his face. Too dark to know what might be reflecting in Chase's eyes, Barry kicked sand. He turned toward the crashing wave.

Chase looked to a Tropicana balcony's light where a figure lurked. Sounding waves drew him to Barry. Resounding crash of surf exploding on sand deafened him. "Damn, you. Goddamn you Barry. Why can't you leave me?' he breathed, grimaced, inhaled a burst of sea air.

Barry slumped to the sand, turned his head to follow the fleeting shadow. Waiting to weep from loneliness, he squinted. A thunderous crash of waves jolted him. Bare feet appeared in the sand. Light above the beach telephone cast an eerie light upon a face. Rising, he looked. No words. A she wrapped her arms around her breasts, shuddered. He reached. She withdrew.

Candace withdrew from the balcony. Tried to find herself in dreams. Emily had never failed to come home, never failed to roll her lower lip in contrition for having acted badly, for having run before thinking. Candace hugged herself. Comforted in knowing she would soon hear Emily's timid knock on the door, the lingering dream of the CNN reporter's questioning dissipating, she sank into the safe dreams of Eyota, of boys calling, of a past when innocence was her trump card, calmed her. Following the football bus to where Eyota's opponent's quarterback appeared in the glare of her headlights unreeled in slow motion as it projected her sleep.

Chase and Barry did not know where fate might lead them while at Saint John's. They had romantic notions that they could swim and dive well enough to qualify for future Olympic competition. They were D-III competitors, yet they still dreamed of becoming Olympians. Why not? Working-out together. Lifting weights and raising egos, who knew how far they might ride their dreams? Father Ambrose had chastised them after they returned to campus to celebrate with too much beer after winning Division III Team Nationals. "Moderation in all things is Godly," he said. "You two must be careful of enjoying too much joy in each other."

"Careful?" they questioned in unison from their shared couch.

"Yes. Careful. Friendship such as yours . . ." his voice evaporated.

"Father, forgive me, but you. You. You. Um. You might sus.

Sus. Um. Suspect too much " Chase stumbled.

Barry's muscles tensed. "Father. Don't worry about us." He popped a beer, poured it into Father's mug. "Cheers!"

"Perhaps a fire. A fire like those we started when you were freshmen, fresh from home, fresh from high school, fresh from parents!" Father Ambrose laughed as he rose and turned to the door of Metten Court's senior apartment.

Arms around shoulders, Barry and Chase swaggered after Father Ambrose to the concrete patio where the fire ring lay surrounded by two-foot stumps. Placid Stumpf Lake lay a few feet beneath. Its muddy bottom discouraged swimmers, but the bridge over the narrows had become part of Johnny-swimmer lore. To stand on its two-foot wide ramparts and piss while they prayed for good grades and good sex was a matter of brotherhood bravery. Chase peeled his arms from Barry's shoulders.

"Race you to the bridge," Chase challenged as he slapped Barry on the back.

"No way you can beat me!" Barry shoved so hard that Chase fell to his knees.

Father Ambrose retreated to the wood box at the side of the apartment. He hoped that Brother Onan had remembered to fill it. The little-bit addled Brother Onan often stuffed the morning paper in the wood box. Stacked the wood on the doorstep. Abbot Paul had admonished Father Ambrose for sending Brother Onan to the woods alone with an axe to chop windfall into cords for the fire rings nestled on the concrete patios of Metten Court apartments. "The man's soul will quickly be on its way to heaven if he misplaces one stroke," Abbot Paul had admonished.

Chase raced Barry to the bridge. Slipped out of his jeans. Stepped out of his boxer shorts. Tossed his t-shirt. "I bet I can piss higher and farther and swim back to shore faster than you can sing the first lines of the alma mater. "Thy Children here today, galore, Old Saint John's! Our dear Saint John's. And true will they be ever more, Old Saint John's! Our dear Saint John's!" Chase screeched.

"Alma mater. What is that?"

Chase slapped Barry's naked ass. "Stop being such a dumb ass!" He had stripped in the few seconds it took for thunder to follow lightning.

Gentle breezes caressed their genitalia as each tried to piss higher, farther and longer than the other. Chase laughed, "Remember when we were sophomores? When we walked the arboretum trails in the winter and pissed our full names in the snow? Think. We won't ever do that again."

"We?" Barry shook his penis. "You did it just to show off your dick."

"And you gazed with wonder!"

"Hey, you two. Stop polluting the sacred Stumpf and get your skinny butts back here," Father Ambrose shouted.

"Take a long look Father. Before I put it to bed for the night."

"You never put it to bed." Barry laughed.

Car lights spotlighted Chase and Barry. Chase flashed the peace sign. Barry turned toward the river. Mooned the car. Father Ambrose shouted, "Damn it!"

Car's horn and shouts of female voices pierced the air.

"I'll show them," Chase shouted. He turned toward them and swayed from side to side like a hula dancer—penis swaying in the light. Barry pushed him into Stumpf Lake. Jumped.

"Oh, sweet Jesus," Father Ambrose muttered to himself. "I will answer to the Abbot.

Horn honking, the car sped off.

Chase and Barry's feet stuck to Stumpf Lake's mud. They wiggled. Free, they bobbed to the surface. Scrambled up the riverbank.

Father Ambrose scurried to ignite a fire. "Damn kids. Tomorrow the Abbot. Damn kids. Tomorrow the Abbot will call. I will. I will," he prayed for an explanation. "Tomorrow God will still love them." He crossed himself.

Chase and Barry rolled onto the concrete patio like spawning fish. Heaped together, they laughed hysterically.

Morning after surviving his Stumpf Lake plunge with Barry, Chase eased out of bed. Stepped barefooted to the cold tile floor. Instinctively he winced from the shock of the cold and the ache of his head. *Shower! No time.* "Damn." A passing grade in senior seminar was required of all College of Saint Benedict women and Saint John's University men. Chase had missed the first week of classes during Division III Swimming and Diving Nationals. Was his grade in jeopardy? Knowing Brother Onan's reputation, Chase knew it might be.

Barry rolled, moaned when he heard Chase's "Damn."

No college senior being of sound mind would sign up for an 8:00 a.m. senior seminar. Barry was smarter. His senior seminar was a night class. He moaned into his pillow, flipped to his stomach and snored to sleep. Chase had registered late. The last seminar open was an eight o'clock. Chase cupped his hands, wet his hair to smooth the cowlicks, ran his fingers through, raked his toothbrush across his teeth, slipped jeans over his boxers, threw on an unwashed red Johnny t-shirt, slammed the door and jogged toward Quad 224. Easing through the door at 7:55, he smiled. *Damned good dash,* he thought.

Slumping into a desk, Chase crossed himself as he remembered his forgotten: pen, pencil, paper, sense. He grimaced, slunk farther into his chair as he splayed his legs beneath the table. He sensed eyes climbed his face. He burped beer stench. Covered his mouth. Hoped he didn't smell of skunk, pulled his legs, body along with it, to a seated position, slowly turned his head to survey the room. Eyes snagged. Hers did not blink. His closed. He felt his penis stir. *Down boy*, he said to himself. It was a mantra he had repeated over the years to quiet himself ever since he had asked his mother before puberty and sex education classes if it would pop up when he didn't want it to. She laughed. "Someday you will hope."

"Gentlepersons," Brother Onan intruded. "Good morning. Good morning soon-to-be-graduates. Good morning soon to be the esteemed alumni and alumnae of our bastions of liberal education. God bless you. Now. You will recall. If not, Mr. Chase? We began last week's discussion by comparing your hopes for your futures beyond graduation from these hallowed institutions—your College of Saint Benedict and your University of Saint John's to the hope of the hopes of the folks who hope hopelessly." Brother Onan chuckled, scratched his nose with his index finger before sliding half-glasses farther down the bridge of his nose, so he could peer into the distant sleepy faces of his captives. Captiva, he digressed in mind and soul. What an island! Wealthy alumni had thrown one hell of a spring break for him and two David and Goliath monks. God would forgive anyone who favored fine wine and scotch and gourmet meals after months of breaking breakfast bread in silence. They swam. They laughed. They threw away old habits for a moment to indulge moderately, always moderately of all things God's good earth provided: lobsters from the sea, mignon from the prairies, cognac from the gods. Divine wine from the wedding at Canaan. Why not displease the creator when offered the finest?

Chase opened his eyes to sneak a peek across the room where he found eyes wide and round enough to drown in. Down and looking up quickly, she smiled. Car light illuminated her first and only vision of a naked Johnny. She loved Johnny swim meets. Speedos. Muscles. Swimmers. Divers. Basketball and soccer boys covered too much. Baseball players looked like they were dressed for a fall walk through the arboretum. She had eyed Chase for the past two semesters, but she was never bold enough to stop outside the natatorium to wait for him. Kellie liked to lurk in the anonymity of crowd. Many girlfriends had all lured Johnnies to their beds and to promises of engagement. She would be bridesmaid to a few. But she felt no panic, no urge to settle. He. There. Limbs she could love to wrap. His eyes flicked to hers. She blinked. Smiled. Lowered her eyes to her text. Put her index finger to her lips.

"Hope graces our campuses, or is it campi?" Brother Onan chuckled. "Hope with its impressive personage has blessed us with insights into human nature," Brother Onan continued. "And no one of you should ever choose not to hope. Have faith when all seems hopeless. Rest always in the arms of hope. Hopelessness leads persons to despair. But hope guides those of us who despair. Our Father forgives if you know not what to do if you lose your grip on hope. But Our Father will find it difficult to forgive if you lose hope. He will not forgive you if you do not give unto others who have no hope even when you are hopeless. There, my precious graduates, lies the essence of the hope we give to you. Hope. You are not alone. You are not lost in the chaos of the unknown. We promise to you, to all of you, when you leave these woods, streams, and halls where your hopes were molded of the clay of the soil of our sacred institutions, fired in the kiln of knowledge consecrated by God," Brother Onan hesitated, tears in his eyes, hope in his heart, words escaping him for the moment. "Always be hopeful. God's hand will guide you."

Had Kellie heard the words? Had the words permeated her being? At this moment in time, she, Kellie, he, Chase—neither would recall words. Images of glistening eyes, entangled limbs, soft images, fleshy odors beguiled them.

Thinking of hope, Kellie glanced again at Chase. Chase's eyes blurred as he recalled Barry tangled in his bed sheet. He squinted to obliterate the image of brotherly love and the relentless locker room stench. *We're brothers here. She, there, close.* He blinked and winked. She smiled. He raised an eyebrow. He wanted to be out. Out of school. Out of the dirty sock man-smell, the sticky wet of dreams. Four years and his social world had been constricted to pool, classrooms and locker room. He understood the athletic world, the ass-slapping, towel-whipping atmosphere where one had no fear of anyone or anything in the world.

"Amen," rumbled throughout the room.

Kellie and Chase found themselves the last exiting through the ten-foot classroom door. Chase nudged the door with his shoulder, held out his hand as a gesture for her to pass. She put her hand in his. Hope?

Chapter 10
Barking at Miramar
Iguanas: Have excellent vision and are able to see shapes, shadows, color, and movement at long distances

Surviving Velas Vallarta, escaping in a cab to Tropicana's beach, Emily stood looking out to sea. She turned toward the light glowing above the pay telephone. It is time. Time to wake up Mother. She rang the Tropicana and asked the clerk to ring her room. "Mom?"

Movement behind her startled her. She gasped. Dropped the phone receiver. Waves crashed, thundered and sent up a spray that wet her hair. She shook her head. "You?" she wiped spray from her face, laughed.

Barry didn't know what to say or do. He felt naked.

"I know you."

"How?" He had never been close enough to her for her to recognize him. Unless?

"Pools." Yes. He's Mother Candace's pool boy. And he was on Chase's swim team. The effects of too much tequila and too little sleep made her head swirl.

"What?"

"Home. St. John's. I thought that was you at Coco." She shivered. Felt cold.

"Oh shit," he said.

"Yes. I knew."

"Yes what? Knew what?" Barry hoped she didn't know more.

"Knew who you were even without your Speedo."

"What the hell?" He thought neither she nor Candace had recognized him at Coco.

"Speedo. St. John's swim team with my brother Chase. You were so sexy in your Johnny red and blue Speedo." She looked up into his face, wet her lips, exposing the stud. "I saw you sitting there at Coco Tropical. Recognized you even without the Speedo!"

"You didn't see me sick. God. I hope not."

"Far too beautiful, you, and, and, ah, Chase didn't say he had two sisters. I remember two pictures on his desk."

Emily tossed her head backward and landed it on his shoulder. "You shit. You know it was Mother and me. Mother who controls all." She shivered. Folded her arms in an attempt to stop shaking.

Barry drew Emily close to his chest. A sea breeze rose. "Come," he said. "I have a place near the flea market. You can crash there."

Emily lifted her head from his shoulder. "Are you safe?"

"Safe," Barry laughed. "I am. And you are. Chase and I thought we were. But now. Beware of the dog." He laughed, squeezed her and thought, *I hope her old man barks bucks.* He began to plot as he gentled Emily past the flea market. Of course she would trust him. He knew Chase. Chase's sister. All were swimming in perilous waters.

Barry huddled Emily close to him as they walked to the south end of *El Centro* between two roads that crossed the Caule River dividing *El Centro* from *Viejo Vallarta*. They turned left to *Miramar*. "Knock until the dog barks," he whispered.

Emily peered up to meld her grin to his. "Are you kidding?"

She knocked.

Barry ran his fingers under her chin. Kissed her.

She flexed her tongue.

"Knock louder," he whispered a laugh.

Emily giggled. Burped. Covered her mouth with the back of her hand, curled it into a tiny fist and tapped.

"That was way too timid. Knock louder. He's older and, ah, sometimes, well, ah, sometimes he sleeps so soundly his dreams mute reality."

Emily giggled. "Quite a watchdog!" She peered at the sign behind the iron-gated door at *Miramar*. Glare from the streetlight hurt her eyes. She pressed her forehead against the cat-and-rat iron grid. She read aloud the childlike scrawl K printed backward—Knock until the dog barks. She turned her back to the gate. "You didn't make that sign. Who are you trying to fool? And why isn't it in Spanish?"

"Too smart, Emily." Barry squeezed her arm and spun her around. "Knock. Knock loudly."

"I, I think. I'm gonna be sick," she said.

"Then knock. I forgot my key. Knock."

Emily stuck her hand through the six-by-six inch square formed by the iron grate and rapped furiously on the white door. She heard a low growl roll forth. She was afraid of stranger's dogs. Feared all dogs except Thorpe's. Bile rose from stomach to throat. Burned. She coughed, collapsed into Barry's arms.

White door edged open. Barry flattened his left hand over her midsection and eased her backward as the iron gate pushed against them.

A deep-throated growl followed by a snarl, a parting of lips and a raucous laughter erupted. "What the hell have you dragged home?" Queen little-fingered the corner of his eye to clear a smudge of mascara. "Let me look. Ohh. Umm. You brought a ripe one!"

Barry honeymooned Emily her over the threshold. "Close the gate. Get me a blanket. Put it on the couch. And a couch pillow. Get a couch pillow."

"Whee and whoa a moment. Aren't we being a bit demanding? Where the hell did you snare her?"

"Sweetie. Just do it."

"In a sec." Queen paused.

Emily's head hung loosely over Barry's arm like a peony blossom.

"I've seen. No. I saw. I saw her."

"What? Where?"

"In the bathroom."

"You've been smokin' again. Get the damn blanket and pillow. She didn't start out to be heavy. But."

Queen flicked his fingers across Emily's brow. Pushed hair from her eyes. "Yes."

"Yes? What? For Chrissakes?"

"Here. Here's the blanket and the pillow. I'll spread it wherever you chose, my little prince. I'd do anything to please you, to lure you into my bed." Queen smirked.

"Shut up. It'll be light soon."

"Okay. Okay. I'll spread the blanket. I'll lay a pillow. Tee hee. Lay a pillow!" Queen giggled.

Emily snuggled against Barry's arms as he folded her into the blanket. She opened her eyes, murmured, and fell asleep.

She awoke to coffee aroma.

"I thought that would wake you," Barry said as he gestured toward the steaming cup. "How do you feel?" He pulled the blanket around her shoulders as she sat up.

"Grubby," she said. She sipped the coffee, setting down the cup and feeling safe but remorseful for what last night had become. "Shower? I need a shower."

"Finish the coffee. Can I fix an egg? Toast?"

"I'm so sorry to have caused so much trouble." She stood and walked the few steps to the make-shift kitchen. A two-burner hot plate with a greasy iron skillet on one burner, a toaster and a one-quart saucepan completed the kitchen cookware. A dormitory-sized refrigerator connected to an outlet by a frayed six-foot cord stood by itself against a gray wall. Emily tried to conceal her surprise at the dismal living conditions, but a surge of anger flashed across her face and nearly betrayed her.

Barry reacted immediately. "I know," he began, but she interrupted him.

"Thanks for taking me in last night. I'm not sure that I ever want to see my mother again."

Barry grimaced. "Whoa. Wait a minute."

"I mean it. I won't be controlled anymore by anyone. Chase escaped. I've been trapped in Wayzata all of my life." She sat down on the lone kitchen chair. Barry propped himself against the table.

"Kiddie beauty pageants. It didn't take me long to realize they were for mother and her friends. Every time she plopped on the lipstick, eye shadow and pinched my cheeks. Every time she curled my hair and painted my finger and toe nails with garish pinks. Every time my stomach ached." She got up and poured more coffee.

Barry was not surprised that Emily's mother would force her to perform just to show her off in competitions Emily could not understand. He understood aching stomachs too. His father drove away from Crosier Prep. Every time Barry thought of that day he could smell the exhaust and feel the ache in his stomach. He wished he knew how to forgive. His revenge was to study hard and make it on his own—without a father.

"Why did you run yesterday?"

"I was crazy with anger. Crazy with hatred for her trying to control me, for making a public spectacle of me one too many times."

Barry moved from the table, stood in back of Emily's chair and put his arms around her. She dropped her head to her chest.

"My dad controlled me with angry words, the same way he controlled mother. I remember the late night startling ringing of the phone. No one ever called us after 9:00 after having endured dad's cursing them for disturbing him so late at night. My friends rarely called, even during the day. We had to do all of our communicating in school or on the bus." Barry stepped back, warmed Emily's coffee and poured a cup.

"That must have been terrible," Emily said. "I don't think my stomach can take any more coffee. I do need to shower."

"Yes. I forgot. Sorry. I'll get you a towel. I hope we have a clean one," he laughed. "And I don't want to wake Queen. He gets very angry if his beauty sleep is disturbed."

While showering and thinking about the call she had made to Candace, Emily began to form a plan to cause her mother a bit more anxiety.

"You look great," Barry said when she returned to the kitchen. "Here." He handed her peanut butter toast on a paper towel. "We don't cook or eat in much," he apologized. "While you were showering, I was thinking. I think I've spent my life trying to figure out my dad's anger. And you spending your life dealing with your mother controlling you." He took an audible breath.

"The angriest I ever heard him was during and after that late-night call. I remember dad saying Dan way too loud. And something about not having enough money to pay, and not giving a shit about him or his money. I didn't discover until I was in college that Dad was talking to your dad."

"Oh, my God," Emily shook her head.

"I have never given up hope that I could find out where the anger came from and still find a way to make Dad respect me. He doesn't respect me because the scholarship from Crosier Prep didn't come close to paying for college. He's always angry about the money I owe." Barry felt a rush of emotion surge through his body that he was afraid might bring tears.

Emily jumped up. "I have an idea. Something we can do that will cause no harm, but, maybe you can pay back your debt with some of Daddy's money and we can both escape our families."

Chapter 11
Long Distance

Iguana's Ear: Is known as the tympanum. It is the iguana's eardrum, and is located right above the sub-tympanic shield and behind the eye. This is a very thin, delicate part of the iguana, and crucial to their hearing.

Jangled telephone rings intruded on Candace's dreams of the quarterback she knew only as "heat." She shook herself awake. Dream exploded into reality. She lay back on her pillow to will herself back to dreaming. The phone slipped from her hands to the bed. She tongued her lip to moisturize. "Mom?"

With trembling hand Candace reached toward the tiny voice. *Where? Where is the phone?* Her mind and hand searched through the confusion of tangled sheets. *Emily. Oh, God.* Frantic hands stumbled onto the cord. She snaked the receiver to her ear. "Oh, my God! Emily?" She twisted the phone cord around her index finger, never wanting to let go. "Jesus! I've been dying to . . . "

"Mom?" Then nothing but the sound of waves and faint voices.

In a panic Candace shouted at the desk clerk to call Wayzata. "You have the number?"

"Si."

"Ellow?"

"Hello. Daniel? Daniel? Wake up! For Chrissakes wake up! I can't hear you."

"Candy?"

"Of course. Yes. Who the hell else would be calling you? Are you sleeping? Drunk? For Chrissakes, Daniel. Wake up Emily. Oh my God, I mean Emily called. She said Mom and then nothing. No more of her voice."

An audible susurration. "Ah. Oh. Candy. You know. We know. Emily's run. She's played her Sarah Bernhardt card one too many times. Why in hell are you so worried? Emily's done this. Done this over and over again. Forever!"

"No, no. This is Mexico. This is the third world. Dopers. My God. May God forbid? Rapists. And if they find out who she is—rape and ransom."

"Calm down. *Puerto Vallarta* is one of the safest cities. It's sea and land-locked, for God's sake."

"Safe? Calm? Calm down? Our daughter!" Candace thought to weep, to stutter, to swallow words to make him listen. "Might. She might." Candace clung to her throat, making her words squeak. "She might be," she gasped, "might be in the clutches of a pervert right here in *Puerto Vallarta*." She tossed her head back. Defiant as a queen dismissing an underling, she accused, "All you can say is calm down!" She inhaled deeply. Commanded in her most imperious voice, "Get on the next plane! Get down here now! Damn it!"

"Candace." He felt he had fended off legions of her imagined villains, only to slay them with promises to protect her and offerings of jewels from Bachman's, when the villains returned time and time again. "Listen. Listen very carefully." He sipped a neat scotch. Placed the glass carefully on the nightstand. "I will not say this again. Again to you. Puerto Vallarta is safe. Emily is safe. Emily is . . ." he picked up his scotch and swallowed. "She is our willful child. She uses us to get her way. This—this one more time is one more time too many. I will not. I repeat." He swallowed the scotch remains. "Listen carefully Candace. I will not play her game this time or any other time in our living future."

Chapter 12
Our Lady

Iguana: Are nearly invisible in the high canopy above Rio Caule

Our Lady of Guadalupe Cathedral is located across the main plaza in old Vallarta. Its interior's white plaster stuns the eye as marble and gold accents reflect streams of sunlight shimmering through stained glass windows. Her bells ring hours, quarter hours, half-hours, three-quarter hours and on the hour. At the altar Jesus opened his hands like a prayer book to receive the host from Padre Jose de Jesus the Divine. Jesus summoned saliva to soften the host as he shuffled from the Father to the last of pews. "Father, forgive me for. . . for forgetting Juanita." Words locked in throat. "I pray for the blonde from el Norte." *Tease. Another tease. I have escaped. Maybe she will suffer for the darkness in her soul.*

Rising from prayer, Jesus signed Father, Son and Holy Ghost. Dipped fingers in Holy Water. Muttered Father, Son and Holy Ghost. Stumbling on Our Lady's steps, he squeezed the light from his eyes. Rather than walk to the bay where the waves' conversation with the rocks might seduce him, he paused. Our Lady's bells rang. He sat. Waited. A five-block's jog to the bay from *Calle Hidalgo* was just a twenty-minute bus ride to home where father would have left for work. Juanita would welcome him to his bed and dreams. She combed her hair in a mirror that always reflected her beauty. Every night with his face covered with his pillow, he found refuge in her peaceful eyes and warm embrace. In eighth grade he had begun to dream of a peek at the flow of her hand brushing her raven hair. He never dreamed of any other, until this blonde from *el Norte*.

Cool air discomfited Jesus. He was accustomed to suffocating humidity, to temperatures that slew natives in August. Jesus shivered, folded his arms, not knowing where to go. His habit was to jog the malecon early and late where the sound of waves would cleanse his mind of the day's thoughts. Jog. Heat to sweat. Get rid of the stench of *Velas Vallarta*, rid of *Nuevo Vallarta*, rid of the blonde from *el Norte*. Fatigued, Jesus lowered his eyes to *Calle Independencia*. A tattoo sign snagged his eye. He craved needles to pierce his skin just above his sternum. Juanita, he would etch on his heart. No shops open. Silver caught his eye in a shop window. He would wait for a ring. For Juanita he would wait. Leave silver to cruise shippers searching for bargains. Leave cheap silver for the blonde from *el Norte*. Soon more tourists would debus, spew khaki-clad, pasty legs topped by waves of gray hair onto his streets. They would finger cotton blankets, some garnished with red fish and silver iguanas. Others would pose before purchasing straw hats they would toss to the garbage at home.

Jesus smoothed hair from his forehead as he jogged toward the pier. Sweat steaming. Thoughts searing. Breath surging. Lungs aching. He burst into a run. Digging feet into sand he flipped his knock-off Nike tennis shoes as he sprinted past Daiquiri Dick's restaurant. *Fired. Fired me for taking pesos from another blonde from el Norte. Why didn't I learn?* He shook his head, the silver cross at his chest swinging wildly. Surging onward, sweat dripping to sand, he raced to outrun his thoughts.

Where has she gone? Why gone from where we could have been together without fear of no man or woman coming between what could have been our dreams of being one in flesh and spirit without shame of colors of skin and hair and love of anything other than ourselves fighting to be one in a circle of peace?

Jesus slipped on a carelessly discarded plastic cup, fell flat on a protruding rock. Aching. Groaning. Rubbing his testicles with throbbing hands, he bent over, grimaced. Cupped his hands around the ache. "Let her go," Juanita warned.

Chapter 13
Flights to Ordaz

Iguana: Have no wings

Puerto Vallarta lies along Banderas Bay, the second largest bay in the Western Hemisphere. It is located 352 kilometers (219 miles) from Guadalajara, the State Capitol of Jalisco, and it is nestled in the foothills of the Sierra Madre mountain range. On Mexico's west coast in northwest Jalisco lies Gustavo Diaz Ordaz International Airport.

Dan's pilot landed the corporate Beech 490. Dan sipped the last of his Glenfiddich, stood to stoop as he exited. "Watch your head," the flight attendant admonished as he crouched into the humid morning air—air that soothed his skin and repressed his urge to tongue-or-lash the luscious flight attendant. He never wanted life to be complicated. Surviving Vietnam, he would not permit lives to spin out of his control. Daughter on the run. Wife always living on the edge. Should he have phoned to let Candace know he was on his way? Thank God for a son who had some sense to escape the madness of home and hearth. Chase had confided to Dan that he would honeymoon in Aruba. Dan assured him he would pick up the check. Chase protested. Something sinister lurked in Candace's call. He would surprise and shock her. He had told her he would not come. Surprise might give him an advantage. Knock. Open. There Candace would stand and possibly fake a faint.

She would be shocked that he had arrived. He had not worried about Emily. He had raised her to be a survivor. He always worried that Candace might not be.

Inhaling the humid tropical air, as Rick stepped down the stairs from the rear of the plane, he rubbed his arms. He glared at the blonde who bumped him in the chest with her elbow as she retrieved her faux-Gucci from the overhead bin. She glared at him beneath black eyebrows. "Screw you, you little cum-squat-on-me," he muttered as he walked from the tarmac to the terminal. This no Vietnam heat. No reason to sweat. He patted his hip pocket. Secured his wallet.

Sun sneaks into *Puerto Vallarta*. Private jets and commercial airliners do not. Rick and Dan had not connected since the middle-of-the-night call Rick made to Dan two years after they had separated from service at Fort Ord. Flying Tiger airlines had dropped them in California where they were welcomed with spit and spite from flower children outside the fort's gate. Dan smiled. He knew he would be welcomed to the family's corporate world. Rick sneered. He knew there would be no parades to welcome him in Hayfield.

In the middle of a muddling night, Rick wove the phone's ring into his dream of soft thighs bringing climax. Rings persisted until he shook himself awake. Stubbed his toe on the rag rug Sharon had thrown on his side of the bed, so he would not slip on the bare floor they could not afford to carpet. "Shit!"

"What?" Sharon woke.

"Phone. Never mind."

Rick knew of no one he cared about who might have died this late at night. Anyone else would have the good sense to call at a— "Hello?"

"Hey old buddy? Is it really you?" *I don't know why I do this.*

"Dan?" *A nightmare voice calling in a dream?*

"Me? You know it's me?" *Always the little man who has to be in control.*

"You're drunk." *Hang up. Hang up.*

"No. Been thinkin' about you though." *He never could talk sober.*

"What the hell is this all about?"

"Always the smart ass, little man. I'm flying down in the corporate jet to Rochester and then on by car to Austin for a meeting with the Hormel people." *Why did I mention the corporate jet?*

"So what's that have to do with me?' *I'll shove the phone up his corporate ass.*

"Lunch. Lunch old buddy. Austin Country Club. Best chef in southeastern Minnesota, I'm told." *Food will get to him.*

"I can't." *Won't.*

"Hey. Don't insult an old buddy. I'm paying." *I'll always pay for the silence.*

"Never. You don't have enough money or conscience to pay." *He forgot me at the gate at Fort Ord.*

"What? What the hell are you saying?" *I can't love and finance everyone from the past.*

"I'm saying I don't give a shit for your money. And I don't give a shit for you. Never did." *Why do I lie?*

"You did. You do." *Why do I owe him?*

"Send me a check, asshole." *I'll chew it up and send it back in an envelope sealed with bloody lips. Maybe toss in a grenade.*

"Stop." *Why the hell is he so angry?*

Someone hung up.

Hang up. Never answer the demands of voices in the night.

If you concentrate, you can manage your nightmares—even the small ones, ones like splashing Cabernet in the general's wife's cleavage. Neither Rick nor Dan ever came close to a general to dream of that opportunity. They knew how to kill. Tell yourself you can wake up from a dream's disaster—kill it. You can will the wine back into its glass. Rewind your dreams. Force your eyes open. Embrace your pillow. Close eyes and see the smooth wine flowing into your hand. Start with small nightmares. Never move on to bigger ones until you have mastered the small. Master the small dreams in anticipation of the huge—the soul-crushing dreams that become nightmares. Recall the screams of babies shot in combat. Compress them. Make them rock and roll to your cadence. Make them screech until Jimmy's guitar squelches them with his rendering. Shape sounds and sights to your will.

Rick had not hung up when the call came from Barry—the call that drove him to call for a flight to *Puerto Vallarta.*

"Dad?" Barry squeezed his ear to the phone. The sound of the waves made it difficult to hear.

"Who? What? Goddamn!" *Calling me at this time of night?*

"Dad. It's me. Barry." He slid his hand into his pocket.

"Barry? What the hell? Where are you? And what the hell are you doing calling me?"

"Dad. I need you." Barry forced his voice to be childlike and contrite.

Sharon got up and stood at Rick's side. "Who is it?"

"Sssh." Rick put his arm over Sharon's shoulder.

"Dad?" *How do I convince him?*

"Yes?" Rick gripped Sharon's arm.

"Who is it!"

"I'm talking to Barry, dammit." He tried to push her away.

Sharon's only thought was for Barry's safety. He rarely called. Even at Saint John's. He was forbidden to call from Crosier Prep.

"Dad. I can get my hands on big money."

"Where are you?" He tried to hold the phone to his and Sharon's ear.

"Puerto Vallarta."

Rick slid the phone to his left ear.

"I said money, Dad. Big money."

"For Chrissakes, Barry. Grow up." Rick pulled Sharon to his side.

"Remember Dan?" Barry knew Rick could not forget Vietnam. He'd seen the pictures in the box of photos in the attic.

"Dan? What the hell?" Rick wanted to crush the phone in his hands.

"The Dan in your Vietnam photos!"

"Photos. What the hell? You snooped in the photos?"

"Dad. Listen! Here. Now. I have his daughter Emily. Money oozing all over her."

"What the hell are you talking about?" He whispered to Sharon, "He's talking big money. Always talking. Stop rubbing my shoulder."

"Your Army buddy is going to pay. Dan. Emily says he has way too much money."

"My God, Barry. Are you crazy?" He pulled Sharon close to him. *"He's crazy. Comes from your side of the family. Stop touching me."*

"Crazy? No. I'm not crazy. We can make this work. I know crap happened in Vietnam. And you lie."

"Lie?"

"Gotta go."

"Barry. Don't. Don't do anything."

Barry cradled the phone far from his ear, looked to a circle of light—light from a hotel balcony. He dropped the phone.

Rick heard gotta go. "Trouble. He's trouble again. Don't." Rick moved toward the kitchen.

"Don't what? Don't touch you?" She closed her robe around her. "You— "

"Don't start. I'm going." Rick turned from her.

"Where?"

"To Mexico. That little shit needs to be stopped. I'm calling for a flight."

"What? You aren't serious." She tried to catch his arm as he twisted away from her. "Leave him alone. Wasn't sending him to Crosier Prep enough? For Chrissakes, when does it end?

Rick paged through yellow for Northwest Airlines. "Yes," he said. "Morning? Nothing tonight?"

"Sir. We have very few flights to *Puerto Vallarta* at this time of year."

"What's the earliest tomorrow?"

"Let me check?" After a long pause the voice returned. "6:00 a.m. Coach fare is $486.00."

"That's way too much money. Oh shit. Book it. Let me get a pencil. 6:00 a.m. Seat 31A."

Chapter 14
Blue Beaches

Iguanas: Can survive captivity—have good senses of hearing, smell, and superb vision.

Emily threw her arms around Barry. "That was smart. No. Smarter than smart. Brilliant."

"Thanks." He kissed her. "I really think we can make this work. But we need you to disappear." He fingered her lips.

"Disappear?" She opened her mouth, curled her tongue around his finger. He cupped his hand in the small of her back and pulled her toward him.

"Yes. I think Queen can help us."

When they told Queen about their plot to fake Emily's kidnapping, Queen threw up his arms.

"Oh my God," Queen swished his fingers through Barry's hair. "Stop. Stop before I cry for joy and intrigue and wealth for all of us!"

"Sssh." Emily and Barry began to laugh. Throwing arms round each other they formed a circle.

"We'd better get ready to disappear." Barry began to worry.

"What?" Queen asked.

"Us." Emily said. "Us. We need to disappear. But how? Where? Better to hide in sight."

"Hide? Flee. Fly. Fo. Fum. Why? Fum what?" Queen

laughed. "I love this game. It's best to hide Emily in plain sight.

"What? How?" Barry squeezed Emily's shoulders.

"My call to Mother. She will call home. He will fly. Will come to quiet her. She commands. He obeys."

"Are you sure?" Barry drew Emily to him.

"Daddy never loses. We can beat him. Make some of his money ours." Emily kissed Barry.

"I have an idea," Queen said. "We three, three males, can check-in for the night at Blue Beaches Hotel." Queen plopped his hands on Emily's head. "But we'll need a hat."

"Hat? What? Why a hat?" Barry pulled Emily closer.

"Ah, sweetie. A hat for Manny," Queen said. "You're so dense, Barry." Queen laughed.

"Blue Beaches? Hat? Manny?" Barry threw up his arms. "Oh. Oh, I get it. Emily disguised. Emily becomes Manny. You think we can make this work?"

"Blue Beaches? Chase told me he invited you to go to Puerto Vallarta for spring break. Is that a place for guys?" Emily wondered if she had said too much.

"Yes." Barry said. "But we were going to make reservations for Los Arcos Suites, but I didn't have the money and I wouldn't let Chase pay."

"Chase was confused. He thought you came on to him. He told me he was disappointed that you wouldn't go to Mexico with him."

"Whoa. Wait. No. Not that way. He said that?"

"I'm gone," Queen said. "I'm not here. I'll get our favorite room." Queen grinned. "Boy. Remember, Emily, you have to look and talk and walk like a boy."

Queen looked forward to the ruse. He loved intrigue and deception. Turning an exaggerated hip swivel and wobble of his back side, Queen pranced up the beach toward Blue Beaches.

"You here. This early? You must've partied most and moist last night and left wanting more," the skinny Blue Chair's desk clerk smirked.

"Hey Silverdildo. You ever known me to disrespect you?" Queen fingered his lips. Tossed aside an eyeful of hair.

"Sweetie! I've never been known to be disrespect or be disrespected by gentlepersons of any age. You want what?"

"Not you, sweetie. The red room."

"Again? And who pays this time?"

"None of your wicked business. Can't you see I am breathless for having jogged all the way here?" Queen heaved heavy breasts. Flicked a smile.

"I can see that you are breathing hard as always. How about room 369?"

"Don't be so damned cute. You know I like bottoms." Queen wet his lips.

"One, two or more keys?"

"Four."

"What?"

"An extra, please? I might get lucky"

"Extras cost more. You know that."

"Even if it's for you?" Queen winked.

"You bitch. Always know how to come on to me."

I just returned from my trip to the Blue Beaches and wanted to post this word of caution. First of all, I'm a gay travel agent and I have traveled the world including Mexico several times and the Blue Beaches does not do our community justice. The hotel over-booked guests all weekend, and sent the over booked guests to some One-star, flee bag [who would flee a flea?] motel along the highway thirty minutes outside of Puerto Vallarta. When we finally got our room at the Blue Beaches, it was in my opinion a scam run by straight hustlers. They have not put a single dime into that hotel. The room had the ambiance of a Mexican jail cell [Reviewer has spent time there of course] and the resort itself was not much better. The TV in the room is broken [can't afford pay per view], most light bulbs are burned out and the light bulbs they do have are the ugly florescent type that help promote the Mexican jail cell ambiance. Internet: Anonymous Post

Chapter 15
Velas Vallarta
Male Iguana: Has three eyes, two penises, and never sweats

Barry, Queen and Emily needed sleep more than each other. Falling into exhaustion's arms, Emily chose a bed without a head next to her. Queen wrapped arms around Barry. Both sighed and snored.

Chase had never known a night when sex was not in his imagining. Morning came upon him suddenly as he slipped his hand to the hip-thrust close to him. Soft skin. Mind confused touch. He caressed smooth skin that brought him peace. He heard a murmur from the past—real or imagined when he lay awake at St. John's Metten Court apartments? He could not separate Barry's rustling in the sheets from the sound of his own groping beneath his sheet to excite himself. He felt cursed. Cursed because nothing satisfied.

Kellie blinked herself awake. Felt the warmth on her hip. Again. Now. Begin again.

Candace turned on her side, sensing the morning's breeze on her loins. Emily's thoughts flew out of control. She pushed a pillow between her legs. Stung with Emily's dash to only God-knew-where, Candace awoke, wanted coffee. *Dan damned well better get his ass down here and take care of my daughter and me. Oh my God, what will I do if she, if he, if they ever trip on the truth? I thought I had buried it.*

Dan was thirsty and hungry. *Velas Vallarta* was not far from Ordaz International. Those who wanted to experience American comfort in Mexico found places such as *Velas Vallarta* and *Los Tulles* to suit their tastes. There they would be comfortable and far away from the Romantic Zone with its squat buildings and cobbled streets with metallic buttons implanted at intersections to slow traffic—Mexican speed bumps. Dan was surprised when Candace gave in to Emily's request to book a room at the Tropicana Hotel in the Romantic Zone. Dan shoved an American twenty into the cab driver's hand. *"Velas Vallarta, amigo."*

Rick's pores oozed Vietnam sweat. He felt it all over again as he stepped from the plane to the tarmac. *Now, what the hell? Where the hell do I find Barry? Stupid. Wasted. I wasted money trying to find him. Wasted. Damn.* No thought of where to go or what to do, Rick ignored all of the yellow-shirted cab hawkers as he walked through the open-air terminal

A cab pulled from the curb. Inside a head turned. No, Rick's mind erased the image. Cab stopped. Eyes penetrated as they had so many years before.

"Rick?"

"No." He turned. You can't. I can't.

A voice attached to body and surged from the cab. Strong hands crushed Rick's shoulders. Rick writhed. His fists and shoulder muscles knotted.

"You. It is. You!"

Rick reached for something to grasp. Anything to pull him away from the stench of Vietnam swirling in his nostrils. Arms embraced him. Staring into eyes that invaded his dreams, he lost control of his will. "Damn. Damn. Damn. You? Here?"

"Come. Come Little Man. Share my cab. Come with me to Velas."

Rick succumbed again to the power of the voice. "Little man" rang in his ears from year's past. Bar in Minneapolis. Fragging the lieutenant. Secrets never to be revealed. All congealed in his throat. Constricting his throat to push back the vomit, he coughed. Swallowed the acid. Sputtered, "Velas? Velas what?"

"Velas Villarta," Dan smiled. "Corporate pays. Room for two."

"No," Rick said.

"Why?" Dan was stunned.

"Because you shouldn't be here."

"Calm down."

"It's not me."

"We can talk about this."

"No."

"Velas Vallarta, *amigo. Gracias.*"

Without will for anything other than suppressing vomit, Rick sagged into the seat beside Dan.

Their history demanded silence. No questions of why here, now, in a present Rick had sworn to avoid. Sons swimmers at Saint John's University. Avoiding, Rick hoped never to see or speak to Dan after the gate at Fort Ord. The image of Dan's departure would never leave the reels of Rick's experiences. City and country created a divide between them as if Gucci and Walmart boots had eternally separated them—survival becoming a recurrent curse. They had studied each other from afar.

Chapter 16

Grenades

Iguana, Pelican, Fish: Brown pelicans fish near the threatening dusk until, on straight-lined wings with bellies full of the day's catch, they stream over Mismaloya cove to roost. DDT had thinned their eggs. Cracked open while they sat incubating. Dirtied their bottoms. Relieved them of parenting. Whose conscience would save them when they could not know what the soiled nests portended?

Dan and Rick sat on high stools at the Velas Vallarta pool bar. Rick had fought Dan-nightmares, Vietnam-nightmares ever since separating at Fort Ord. Dan had learned to control his dreams, could wake himself at will to rise to consciousness. He could rewind, expunge, extrapolate, embellish and wake to a life others had created for him. Rick swallowed the bile of the Dan rising.

"Here?" Dan sank his eyes into his Glenfiddich.

Rick rimmed his fingers around the crown of his bottle of Corona.

"Why? What? What the hell are you doing here?" Dan sipped his 'Fiddich. "*Senor.* This tastes of weeds from the shores of Lake Minnetonka! The bottle. Please. The bottle."

"*Si senor*. Here. It says. Glenffiddich." He slid the bottle across the bar to Dan.

Rick felt blood rise to burn his cheeks. *You arrogant son of a bitch. I've escaped your ego for all these years. Knowing our sons were together at Saint John's. Knowing you would be there for every swim meet, I never saw Barry swim. He never questioned. Driven by your Mercedes' ego, you were there. I couldn't let Barry compare me to you.*

Dan smirked. "*Senor*. The real stuff has one less eff. You are serving a knockoff." He turned to Rick. "Great to find you here after all these years. Cheers."

The bartender stood on tiptoes like a matador. Pivoted on his heel. Reached beneath the bar. Gentled a newfound fifth of Glenfiddich next to Dan's glass. Set two glasses. "Enjoy *amigos*," he grinned

Dan poured the Glenfiddich on the bar. "*Uno mas*. Real this time. Run a tab," he commanded.

What the hell am I doing? He's doing it again. Always controlling. Leaving Fort Ord he controlled. Hustling back to daddy and the business. Never gave a shit for me. "What are you doing here?"

"Came here to pick you up. You never showed up as my best man!" Dan said with a laugh followed by another gulp of scotch. "Seriously. Candace phoned."

"Candace?" Rick said. "Candace here? Your Candace. Mrs. Eyota's Candace?" Barry chugged his Corona. "Fill me up with a 'Fiddich scotch," he ordered the bartender.

"What the hell do you know about scotch or Candace and Eyota?"

"*Amigos*?" The bartender raised his eyebrows. "Please not so loud."

Dan waved his hand in the air as if brushing away an annoying fly. "Put the admonition and the scotch on my tab."

"Candace? Eyota?" Rick said. *Now we'll see who has control.* "Uh," he paused. "Football."

"You lightweight. You ingest a beer and a scotch and you go crazy on me?" Dan waved two fingers in a circle above his head. "Football? What the hell? Candace, crazy with anxiety, thinks Emily has been kidnapped and I'm sitting here talking about football?"

"Yes. Football. Eyota. Hayfield." Rick tasted revenge. Years of paranoia of what Dan might tell had eaten too much from Rick's core. Never free to raise the curtain to reveal the drama that he and Dan had scripted and acted in Vietnam had crippled him. Fragging a sadistic lieutenant. Carrying that home to his bed, his business, his little town where nobody spoke of the carnage they saw in their newly purchased color televisions on credit. Everyone overdosed on combat footage. But they could turn it off after the news. Eyota's hardware store had a deal with RCA to sell color and black and white at a discount while throwing in an antenna with rotor for no cost. Perhaps that ended the war.

"I don't give a shit about football, Eyota or Hayfield."

Rick tapped Dan's shoulder. "Hey buddy. You don't want to hear about Candace. Your Candace? I promised myself I would never tell you when you asked me to be you best man. She made quarterbacks way before she made you." Rick dug his fingers into Dan's biceps." He released his hand and curled it around his glass of scotch. They moved to pool side chaise lounges.

"Cheers!" Rick said. "I made quarterback and cheerleaders!" He tossed the scotch to the back of his throat. Rick lay on his side. Curled his knees toward his chin. His breath reeked of stale scotch. He could not sense that anymore the old habit, not quite fetal, yet never protective enough, would stop dreams from exploding beyond his control. Again he lay too near the power Dan held over him.

Rick's early morning dreaming locked him between waking and awakening. Would he ever escape? He loved his son but could not love himself. He had thought he loved Candace that night after Hayfield's football victory over Eyota. Cheerful in her white knit sweater with maroon and gold E letter awkwardly askew against her breast, she stood beside the team bus and waved at his swollen face as it faded into darkness.

There were no locker rooms near the Eyota football field. Opposing schools agreed to play on the eighty-yard field even though the Minnesota State High School League would not sanction games played there. This would be the last year nine-man football would be played in Eyota. Crowds stood six-persons deep on the soggy grass not ten yards from the trickle of creek near U.S. Highway 14. Recurring spring floods spewed nitrogen rich fertilizer from farm run-off to burnish the turf to an emerald green. Players were bused to the high school, a mere six blocks to the south of the emerald green.

Showered and fresh from the lust of victory, Rick threw his arm around his best friend's neck, pulled his head downward in a playful grip.

"Damned good win," Rick said.

"No shit, little beaver."

"We," was all Rick could utter. There, standing by the bus, hands on hips, she stood. Lips pouting.

"Hi." She licked her lips.

Rick stared with open mouth. Turned his eyes and head toward his toes in sweet embarrassment.

Years tossed Rick and Dan together like rocks in a bag in

Vilas Velas. Neither would let the other know he had winced from the painful emotional bruises they had inflicted on the other. Rick hated Dan's arrogance. Dan envied Rick's savagery. Why are moths attracted to burning light?

Rick smelled coffee.

"Perked and ready," Dan said as he poured his. "You?"

Rick stretched legs to bed's edge. Hoisting the pillow from his face, his dream of coffee with Candace evaporated. Trying to will dream to reality, he mumbled, "Score. I scored." Farted. Groaned. "Black." Farted again.

"For Chrissakes. You mumble. Scored? What the hell? You stink. It's Vietnam all over again. How the hell did we survive?"

Rick threw off the bedclothes. Hunched upon his knees and muttered, "Fuck you."

"Relax." Dan poured coffee. "Drink."

Rick pulled sheets over his hairless chest.

"Yesterday," Dan began.

Rick rolled to the edge of the bed. He liked his coffee thick and black. No cream. No sugar. He sipped. Curled his lips into an O of disgust. Thin. Coffee meant for church basements but not meant for atheists. He spat it into the cup. "A fancy place like this ought to have a ceramic mug. Paper cup? You paid for this shit?"

"You little shit. Drink up and shut up. Yesterday you muttered something about Candace."

Must have sunk into his psyche. Now Rick sensed a cudgel in hand. He had never felt as smart or as rich or as smooth talking as Dan, yet now, in this moment he felt equal. No. Not equal. Superior. Whether he and Candace had ever finished what she had started after the football game, Rick would never say. Whether it was dream or real, it did not matter. Power. He could tease Dan with reality or fantasy about Candace. Either would become truth depending on how he narrated the story. He had to decide which version would exact the most revenge. He could blow up the room and explode past and present between him and Dan. Knowing that gave him control. "Candace moaned."

"What? What the hell?"

"Maybe it was a scream."

"Scream?" Dan swabbed sweat from his forehead with his sleeve. "Moans! Screams!"

"Grenade." *That ought to make him shiver*, Rick thought.

"Oh cut the shit. Grenade? Are you crazy?"

"The grenade. You called it heroics. All I could see was military court marshal and death. Death. Mine. You alive. I still hear the moans."

"Whose? Grenades? Candace? Moans?"

"You don't want to know."

"No. None of that. Talk to me." Dan sat on the bed.

"Get away from me."

"Why?"

The Velas: Internet post by slaybelle

The Velas Vallarta hotel is about a two-minute drive from the airport, a thirty-second drive to the Marina Vallarta (definitely a cool place full of ethnic restaurants and shops), and it's about a five to ten-minute drive to downtown Puerto Vallarta. For solo travelers, this place is extremely safe. You're outside of the downtown crowds, but there are also a good dozen hotels in the area, so you're not alone. The staff was extremely friendly, and there are always people there to meet.

Chapter 17
911

Disconnections: The iguana's tail actually has multiple purposes. It can be used to deliver a very powerful strike to predators, and also, it's a defense mechanism. Like many lizards, the iguana has the ability to drop a portion of its tail off so it can escape while the predator eats the tail

Potential plots swam through Emily's subconscious while she, Barry and Queen lay tripled to backsides like spoons in their Blue Beaches room. Red light roaming through the curtained room infused her surreal dream. Caught between the half-light of awareness and the blood-red of nightmare, she willed herself awake. Tried to roll her body aside from nakedness. Paralyzed in sleep, she fought her dreams with her will to awaken to bathe in the light summoning her eyelids to wake. Startled upright, struggling to obliterate the dream, she squeezed her eyelids and forced her body from paralysis to toilet. With a soft hand shutting her dream's door, she blinked. Looking into the mirror, she thought, *I can be a boy. I can escape this madness.*

Needing a binding for her small breasts, she gnawed at the edge of a bath towel. Her teeth hurt, but she was determined to make it work. Saliva spent, she filled her mouth with water from the tap, scissored her teeth until she managed a small tear in the cotton. She ripped a six-inch-wide strip from the towel—bound her breasts.

Afternoon came before Queen and Barry awoke. Bucketed beer on the beach wasted their afternoon. Emily was one of the few on the beach who sported a t-shirt. Her hope of being undiscovered lay in her boyish physique and safety lying between Queen and Barry on the red bedspread that they had sneaked from their room. Crowds would be so dense and non-confrontational that she knew she could hide. *How? How to know?* Safety lay in numbers. She had never felt entirely safe anytime in her life. Now she had found refuge from her mother's nails. Tearing away, she had sprinted to the malecon. Safe until Jesus slipped her into bed at *Velas Vallarta*. And now Barry. Barry she could trust. And Queen. Queen would never harm.

Jesus was exhausted. Emotion spent. "Sleep, bring me to my sense of self," he implored. In the corner of his mind his Juanita combed her hair in his dream-mirror. Image dissolved black to blonde. A crescendo of guilt-want and wet dreams black-and-blonde overwhelmed him.

Flesh-starved, sleep-deprived Jesus walked and jogged and jogged and walked until he reached his family house in the swell of hill beyond the towering turrets of Los Tulles Resort. His family's small patch of property baked in the searing heat while patrons of Los Tulles sank feet into lushly watered grasses and slipped tanned torsos into bikinis. This day he would wrap his arms around his pillow to sleep minutes away before his day job at Hotel Tropicana.

Kellie wanted coffee. She ran her fingers across Chase's spine. Reacting to a muscle twitch, blood rushed to her cheeks. He sighed, curled his knees to his stomach, fetal and vulnerable. "Chase?" she whispered as she breathed softly into his ear. "Love?"

He craned his head toward her. Still, he lifted heavy eyes toward her.

"I'm going to shower," she said. "Sleep and I'll wake you when I'm ready. We have to meet the bus at eleven."

He cupped his hands over his ears. "Eleven? Bus? What?"

She slapped him gently on his butt. "The jungle canopy excursion. Remember?"

"Ahh. No. I can't. We can't." He sat upright.

"What? Why? What are you talking about? My honeymoon gift to you, Tarzan." She raked her fingernails gently inside his thigh. "I booked the canopy excursion when we decided we'd honeymoon here."

"You didn't tell me." Chase snaked his fingers around hers. Aroused. He flipped violently—topping her. Scent of Polo consumed him. "The bus can leave without us."

Candice wound the sheets as if to mummify. A night of beach visions morphing into bitter hammers of words for a husband who would not come to help chase down a daughter who had disappeared into yet another nightmare exhausted her. Candice craved warmth in the arms of an imagined past where there was no chaos. A pool boy. A lemon martini. A ride in the float. Mrs. Eyota in the Eyota day's parade. Eyes of studs pressed upon her. Emily. *Call. Call me. Damn Dan.* A massage. Needing a massage. Needing a man's rough fingers sinking into the deep of her toned body, she thought of her high school quarterback. She rang the operator.

"Hola."

"English. English please," she gritted her teeth. "I need to telephone the U.S."

"Si. Number please?"

"Look it up. It's on my registration card!" Candace was not accustomed to do for herself what others could do for her."

Si. Uno momento."

"Si. I see. Coffee. Send up some coffee, see? While I wait." Candace swiped away a wisp of grey hair that stuck to her lip. *"Gracias."*

Drone of dull phone rings seeped into her consciousness. *Same time. Same zone. Not too early to call. Would he come? No. He wouldn't. Business day. More underlings to make or destroy. He loved it.*

"Hola."

"Maria?"

"Yes."

"This is your Mrs."

"Si?"

"Connect me to our Mr., please—uh—*por favor."*

"Si."

Why didn't Dan hire proper British servants or at least someone from Eyota, or even better, one of her high school classmates who could at least speak English? She rubbed Clarins Moisture Quenching Hydra Balance Cream into her degrading face while she waited.

"Ello?"

"Yes. Yes. *Hola* or whatever?" Candace fingered her lips. Dry.

"No. Mr. Dan not here."

"Not there?" Candace shuddered. "Then where?"

"I will look."

Candace bounced her head against the plastered wall behind the bedstead as she began to laugh hysterically. "Don't look in the bed." Her lips hurt. Her stomach protruded. He might be coming. Here. Jet. Corporate. Anytime. Anywhere. Always the jet was ready for him. He would try to catch up to her whenever convenient. And she knew how to steer him.

"Ello? Miz Candace?"

"Yes, Maria?"

"I look everywhere. No Mr. Dan."

Dispirited for this of several times in her life, Candace ached for Emily's arms, Chase's smile, Dan's hands to wrest her away from the fear of being alone. Coffee, yogurt and a banana had sufficed for brunch. Staying slim exacted its price. She recalled printing names on gift tags for Christmases past. Her childish scrawl on the tag for daddy's tie, for mother's bottle of scent of lilac. She knew if she savored and practiced how simple living and loving could be, she would not have become a trophy. What if she had stayed in Eyota?

Indulging her sense of pity by draping her dreams beneath the twilight of her eyelids, she lay on the bed. Emily always ran away from conflict. Candace hoped two years of college would have cured her of that. She gulped a room service margarita delivered in a plastic pool cup. "Plastic. For God's sake! And I ordered coffee!" She turned to the phone. Stared. Eyes blank. Mind racing from Emily's rush toward the crash of malecon waves, she squeezed the runaway image beneath tightened eyelids until her temples ached. She rubbed fingers on the veins pulsing above both ears. Rang room service. "Coffee? Where the hell is my coffee?"

"*Si.* Soon."

Candace lay back to feed her libido. Pity nestled close to her ego. From the depths of the swamps she had waded through, libido rose: Rick seeking, hardware owner luring, pool boys rising. She pulled her mind to the surface, punched O on the room phone.

"*Si?*"

"English, please."

"Yes."

"Dial 911," Candace joked. "I need to be rescued."

"We have no 911."

"Si," Candace sighed. Of course. No joking in this language. "Just deliver my coffee, pronto!" Candace looked to the door as it wobbled with the knock.

"Yes, madam. *Uno,* ah, one. One *momento.* Please? I make the order again."

"Come, come in. Door's unlocked," she shouted in response to the rattle and knocking reverberation of the door. She'd never had room service this fast, not even at the Waldorf. She got up after a slight hesitation, leaned her eye into the crack of the door opening.

"Mother?" Chase nearly dropped the tray of ginger coffee. Liquid swarmed to cups' lips. Dribbled to the tray. "Here? You? In my room?" his voice squeaked. "Kellie?" he shouted.

"Kellie?"

Overwhelmed with confusion, Candace folded her arms to cover her breasts. "Kellie? Chase! What?"

Chapter 18
Athena

Iguana: Do not wound or kill an iguana in Puerto Vallarta

A mercyful sun would not shed any more light on human's wounds. The iguana warms and swells in the sun, not unlike tropical teens and aging queens who shiver and shrivel in the low-lying northern sun. In her habitat the iguana is disguised from eyes of predators—animal and human. Emily knows. Barry hopes. Jesus trusts Juanita. Chase lies. Dan taunts. Rick fragments. Candace disguises.

"Um," Emily rolled onto her side. "Time? What's? Rest. I need a nap." Warmth slid around her shoulders, nestled between her thighs like a summer breeze. Emily had discovered she could control the light in a dream. Reach and try to turn it off. If it stays on it will become a nightmare. Speaking slowly with words sparking in her brain, each syllable swirling, bursting into a blaze of understanding, Emily drew her knees to her wrapped breasts.

Queen's tender touch soothed her awake. "Sweetie? Wake up. Enough nap. You were great on the beach. No one tried to hit on you while you lay between us. Now we have to get up for the evening. Party's starting soon. It's balloon-popping night. Hilarious."

Emily stroked Queen's warm hands.

"Don't be afraid my lovely. Tonight we party."

Barry awoke. "Shower's mine," he said. "Wake up, Emily. Gonna be a night you'll never forget. Too bad Chase isn't with us."

Emily raised herself on her elbow. Curled her tongue to swab her teeth. *Too much*, she thought. *Out. Need to get out. Barry! Get us out of here. Can't. Won't. No more. No more. Phone? Run? Tropicana close down the beach. But why back to Mother's claws? No. Will Barry hold on to me?*

"Here," Queen said. "Got this from a little boy next door while you were sleeping. "Looks like a perfect fit. And with a little sock in your crotch," Queen snaked his tongue over his upper and lower lip. "Gonna be great fun. Great laughs. You can do the gorgeous-twink thing." He tossed his head backward. Looked at her. "Oh my God! Even I could take you home."

"Spandex? You want me to wear red Spandex? Bind my breasts and wear red Spandex? Stuff a sock in my crotch? Oh, my God!" Emily slid her legs to the side of the bed. "Why not? Why the hell not? Give me a shot of your tequila"

"YMCA" lyrics screamed from speakers scorching the ears of guy-gyrations when Emily, Queen and Barry elbowed through the sweating crowd. Hips swinging, lips simmering, a twenty-something fresh from the shower and glistening with baby oil stood on his hands. He spread his upraised legs in a Y.

Emily slipped away from the crowd. Images of Jesus' flourishing a napkin, the glow of his skin granted her a few moments of peace in the chaos of Blue Beaches' dancers. She pushed her way among sweating bodies as she approached the bar to order straight tequila.

The crowd surged and roared near to the dancer. The circle tightened. Lookers leapt onto tables to see what they could see. His legs dipped, formed an M—circled—swung to the right to form a C. Flipping quickly and expertly to his feet he pulled down his pants to display the climactic A. Thunder inundated the room.

Emily wanted to escape. Tropicana was not more than one hundred yards away. She'd had enough of the charade. She'd forgotten the purpose. She had punished Mother enough. It was time to forgive her. Barry. She couldn't abandon Barry. She pushed aside a sweating twink near the bar, nearly knocking off his cowboy hat. She needed a drink to clear her mind. From the mass of sweating bodies, a face met hers.

"You? Here!" A voice grabbed her arm. Hands covered her mouth. "You look the same as when you were twelve." He forced her head downward until her head hit her knees. Breathe. Her mind screamed! Breathe.

The voice covered her mouth to let her breathe through her nose.

Florid eyes savored the sight of the shaved A of the dancer. Wild screams, clapping and chants of "Young Man Come Again" blared from loud speakers. Barry longed for the safety of the college locker room, for the teasing locker room talk that bound buddies together. Barry looked for Emily. Warm-wet from an arm wound around his neck forced Barry's eyes to turn.

"Ted," the voice attached to the outstretched hand said. "What you drinkin'?"

Trying to slip under the arm, Barry crouched, hoping the arm would slide away. "Not drinking right now."

"Stand up big man," Queen said to Ted. "He's mine tonight."

Barry rose from waist to stand as Ted's arm slid from his shoulder.

"No offense, buddy. Sorry," Ted said as he oozed into the crowd.

"Thanks." Barry turned to push through the massed bodies

surging to chaotic rhythms. *Drink? Emily? Where? She's so tiny. There?* He blinked as lights strobed. White and black images jangled nerves. Queen evaporated. *Emily?* He closed his eyes. Wished reality into a dream from which he would awaken or was this a dream where he could awaken to a reality he could not control?

Barry went to the bar and ordered a fifth margarita. Tequila was so thin at Blue Beaches he could suck up seven or more and still keep his wits intact and his feet under him. Sweat glistened from swollen pectorals. He surveyed the crowd for Emily. Every gyrating dancer looked like his swim mates at Saint John's after shaving for regional competitions. Not a body hair lurked anywhere to the visible eye. *Where the hell is Emily?* His eyes scanned the room. *Where? There.* Queen had consummated his quest. A skinny blond huddled against Queen's feathered bosom. *Where is she?* Barry's mind throbbed.

He elbowed his way through the crowd. Grabbed Queen's neck. "Give up the blond, sweetie. We have to find Em," he paused. "Manny."

"Oh don't be so theatrical." Queen kissed his blond.

Little blond fingered Queen's cheek. Looked up and down."You leaving me for him?"

"No, sweetie. He's my roommate. Nothing happening there." Queen bent his head backward. "Let go my neck."

"Sorry," Barry said. "Where is Manny?"

"Manny? Oh? Yes. Forgot. Sorry. You hot for Manny? You can't have our room," Queen grinned, sipped a melting margarita rock from the blond boy's lips.

Barry released his fingers from Queen's neck. "Sorry sweetheart, but don't bring the boy home. You will upset this puppy!"

"You go home. We . . ." Queen grabbed the blond boy's

buttocks and clean-jerked him toward the ceiling. "We have the red room."

"We have to find Manny."

She's not your type," Queen grinned. "No more than you are mine." With fingernails sequined with gold glitter Queen twirled the little blond's curls around his finger.

Little blond's seascape eyes flooded Queen's senses as he looked up at him.

"Swing me," he said.

Queen laughed. He tossed the blond over his head like a marionette. "See," he shouted to the crowd that had gathered. "See my little magic flutist. He plays the five-finger flute and I am Queen of the tunes he will play!" He twirled the little blond above him, flipped him across his midriff and toted him to the lobby.

"Wait," Barry grabbed the little blond's leg. "Wait."

Queen turned. "Hands off my guy."

"Sure. Sure. You can have your guy. The room. Gotta find Manny."

"Be careful," Queen turned heel and swished toward the red room.

"I need a drink," Barry said as he leaned his elbows on the bar, cheeks in hands. "Two hundred peso tip if you . . ."

The sumo-sized bartender rolled his eyes. "No, man. No favors or conditions."

"No. No. Sorry man. I didn't mean . . . ."

"What are you drinkin'?"

"Nothin' if you can tell me if you saw my little friend. Red Spandex capris. Tiny. As sweet and soft a face as you've never seen. Two hundred pesos?"

"You sweet to chase that?" the bartender turned away.

"Four hundred?"

He turned toward the big man in Army fatigues pounding the bar and yelling, "I need a drink!" The Bartender roared, "You'll get another when I'm ready. I'm busy here." He turned to Barry, "Red Spandex capris?"

"Yes!" Barry smoothed peso notes on the bar, avoiding the smear of beer as he slid them toward the bartender.

"Yah, sure. Older guy. Big tipper. Went off with a skinny little kid in red capris. Old guy's been here many times."

"Old big tipper? And the little guy? You screwing with me? Me and my money?"

"Irony," the bartender swabbed his forehead with a bar rag. "Shut up!"

"I . . ." Barry began.

"Not you. It's the screamer. Here for a month every year." He hoisted a pitcher of iced water and drank it dry. "The red capris."

Barry tired of the verbal sparring. "I'm ready."

"Got another forty pesos?" The Bartender stretched his massive palm toward Barry.

"When you finish."

"When I begin, mother."

"Yah. Yah. Here." Barry riffled soggy pesos from his thigh pocket. Always kept a wad of cash there. He crumpled the sweaty pesos into the bartender's outstretched palm.

"I already told you. Old guy. Been here many times. Always leaves with the smoothest skins he can find. He bent the little red capris' head down. Might have said something." The Bartender scooped pesos into his shirt pocket—deep enough to hold many more.

"You see them leave?" Barry's heart forced its way to his throat.

"No. I didn't pay much attention. Seen it all before."

"You homophobic?"

Cabbies lined the curb. They knew to see and to say nothing. Blue Beaches fares were generous. And what they did or where they went, no meter would reveal. Plentiful pesos paid for ignorance.

"Velas Valllarta *por favor.*"

Through *Amapas* cattle-shoot street they bumped along over rough cobbles. Emily squirmed. Hand over mouth caused her to cough. He pinched her nose. Whispered, "You shouldn't be here. Blue Beaches. What the hell are you doing? Trying to be a boy?"

Turning on *Pulpito* the cab swerved toward the rising sidewalk. A screech echoed as the cab's fender scraped and broke cement.

At *Olas Altas* he tapped the cab drive on the shoulder. *"Alto."* He paid the fare. Wrapping Emily into his arm, hand covering her mouth, he whispered, "If you utter one word I will feed you to the ocean.

If he would harm her, all faith in past and promise of future would no longer be hers. She could escape this. Now. She could. The voice. She knew the voice.

He waved another cab. The highway to Mismaloya was a few blocks ahead. Did he need another diversion? No. No Cabbie would talk even if he did remember.

What would he do with her now as he approached the gate to his condo?

Emily leaned against his shoulder—feeling safe in the arms of this man she had known since childhood. "Tired," she murmured.

"You can sleep here. But you must forget where you saw me tonight. Erase it from your mind." He stoked her cheek. "Then everything will be okay."

A blue and white ceramic plaque illuminated by a gaslight greeted her. "Knock until the dog barks"

"Knock!" he ordered.

Images flooded her seeing. Gibberish muddled her mind. *Why is he here?* Everywhere she felt like a child.

"Knock."

She knocked. An inhuman roar assaulted her ears. A guttural snarl. Thorpe pushed the door. A Doberman jumped to slurp his face, backed off and wagged its tail. Slurped Emily's face.

"Athena," Emily cooed as she scratched Athena's ears. You trying to guard a warrior here, wise one?" She laughed. "I know you wouldn't attack a bone, much less me." *I can out-talk, out-maneuver Thorpe. I know things he won't want anyone to hear. He won't harm me. Maybe he wants more of Daddy's money? But he fears more than anything that I will tell about Blue Beaches. Blow his past and present. He won't harm me. I sense Barry wants me. But Barry has no money. Everybody wants Daddy's money. Except Jesus.* Her mind cast a line she didn't want to throw. It reeled in a memory of Jesus in the Temple. He threw out the money mongers. Did he curse them? *No use,* she thought. *No use for money here. Could she trust anyone? Jesus? Barry? Where are you? Always I have to fight myself to save myself.*

Amanda, Thorpe's demanding daughter, had talked Thorpe into getting her a puppy when she was in high school. Emily had pleaded with Thorpe to persuade her dad to do the same. "We need watchdogs," the girls chimed. A shy Doberman pup jumped and barked in her cage in the Hennepin Avenue animal shelter near the Gay Nineties Bar. Wagged her tail. A year later, after Emily and Amanda had tamed the Doberman, she, being nearly full-grown, became an expatriate in the state of Jalisco.

Run, she thought. *I can always run. Run? Me? They have always run me. Big Daddy and Mommy Candace always on the Twin City social pages. Running the race to society's pinnacle.*

Looking on from the frothy curtains of her bedroom, even Emily knew what mystery lurked behind the stretching fabric of the pool boy's Speedo. First time she could remember seeing her mother naked. She did not understand the talk about filters. The word was strange to her—as strange as her mother's behavior had always been. But now she wanted Barry.

Images flooded her mind and the odor of talcum powder lingered in her nose. With a sudden hip twist and a pout of lips she saw mother twirl toward the pool boy, pressing her nipples to his. He reeled backward, falling heavily onto the concrete. Emily peeled her eyes at the erect penis as it escaped the Speedo. Had mother seen it before?

Call. She could call Amanda. She knew the number. Easy to call from Mexico. *Amanda home? Maybe not? Maybe yes? Maid? Possible. Leave a sign? Leave a clue? But this sorry lump of a man would not, could not harm her simply because she might tell she had seen him at Blue Beaches. No? Yes? No? Safe? No! Where to run if not safe here? Call Amanda!*

Amanda. Best friend. Amanda. Home? Home? Home now? No zone difference. Maybe. Amanda, God, help me, my best friend, help me. Screwdrivers made them giggle. Drops of orange vodka dribbled from Amanda's bangs to her forehead. The screech of mother's voice still echoed. Wet of blood. Emily slow-motion stumbled through the garden door as she ran.

Thorpe grabbed her wrist in the instant after the phone disconnection. "What are you doing? Who would you? My God. Why would you? Listen. Listen carefully. We are adults—you and I. Your mother will never be anything more that the prom queen she never was. Mrs. Eyota, of course. Everyone knew she was no queen. But you, you wear the family's Miss Princess tiara. Your father screwed me out of millions after I was forced from the Minnesota Supreme Court. He was the he, little princess, the he who was screwing my wife. The Minneapolis paper never followed that because none of us would talk."

Emily glared at him. "Let go of my wrist."

Thorpe cupped his hands on her cheeks. "Look," he said as he appealed to her eyes and conscience. "I never intended." He paused, removed his hands. Squatted on the tile floor next to the leather couch where Emily had sunk.

Smart, she thought. *Be smart*. She sat on her feet. Rocked like a monkey. *Tears. Make tears.*

"Daddy's mean." She squeezed a tear. Gasped. Rubbed her eyes with her wrist. "Here," he said. He wiped her face with his shirt cuff. She leaned her head into his shoulder. He folded his arms around her. She felt no fear. He had been at Blue Beaches. No interest in molesting her, she was certain. *Protection. Seize on that,* she thought. "Daddy," she began. Her mind raced for a story that he would seize. She offered him a prolonged sigh.

"Did he hurt you?"

Cry. Force the crying. Tears burst.

Chapter 19
Scotch

Iguana fact: Are you prepared to give this fellow a portion of a room in a couple of years when he grows beyond your capacity to handle him?

"What?" Rick asked as he gulped bitter coffee. "Tropicana? Why?"

"Yes. We're leaving now. It's time to surprise Candace," Dan reached the dregs of neat scotch from the glass bedside table. Its burn blurred the clock. Dan shook his head clear. He drank. "I want to catch her unawares."

"Candace? You'll never catch her that way. I never did."

"Hello? Yes. A cab. Now. Front door. Tell him to wait for a big man and a little guy," Dan tipped his glass to Rick.

"You asshole. Once an asshole—always an asshole."

"Give it up. Forget. Get rid of your goddamed anger." Dan tossed the paper cup to the bed. It bounced and lay dribbling on its side.

"You," Rick tried to swallow bitterness of the past. "You, you walked through Fort Ord's gate. Back to your fortune. I hope you carried the grenade I tossed into your tight little-ass psyche. Nobody ever got into your head. Secure. You. Always secure. Carry this, you big asshole. I screwed her before you ever knew her—your Candy."

124

If the air between Rick and Dan could shriek, it would erupt with the silent roar of "The Scream" and the imagined stench of "Guernica."

Now, Rick thought, *for once in Dan's sorry-assed life, I have his attention.* "Now shut up. Shut the fuck up. Remember Bruckner?"

"Bruckner? Candy?" Dan sat on the bed's edge.

"Oh shit. I should've known. Should've known then. Should know now how easily you forget. Got any more of that expensive scotch you so smugly sip?"

"I called a cab. It's waiting. What the hell are you babbling about? Bruckner? Candy?"

"I said. You got any more of that expensive Candy, ah, I mean scotch?" Rick gulped. "Wanna talk about Candy, Bucks or scotch?" Rick settled into a wingback chair, put his feet up on the hassock and held out his cup. Control. Now he had control. "One more scotch for the road?" He had had no control since the catharsis he had felt after fragging Buckner. Dan's words exploded with the fire of combat in Rick's nightmare: "Poor son of a bitch," Dan had said. Then he thought Rick meant Bruckner.

"You meant me," Rick snarled, one hand on the back of his neck, the other pointing to the scotch.

Dan's eyes' ballooned. *Why? Why did I let this little shit bore into my psyche? I vouched for his age when he didn't have a hair on his smooth little ass at the bar after induction. He sure had hair on his balls when he fragged Buckner. He never did shave during that whole year in Vietnam that I ever knew of. Best man? Shit. He said it was the snowstorm. Bullshit.* "What?" Dan poured two fingers of scotch into Rick's coffee cup. "What the hell are you talking about? You meant me?"

Phone rang. Rick sat up. They locked eyes. Neither moved. "Sure. You and your corporate pedigree, you, you don't remember a thing. I relive it every night." He gulped and savored a taste of grass.

Dan swirled scotch. Peered into the golden glow. Paused long as he dare. Phone rang. Neither moved. "What? Relive what?"

"You shit. You unforgiveable, arrogant shit. I killed him and all you said was, "Poor son of a bitch. Me. Not Buckner. Me! Me! I am the poor son of a bitch. You held court-martial and my life or death in your hands."

"Answer the fucking phone," Dan slurped scotch. "Don't tell me about Candy. You think I'm that naïve' you little shit?" Dan said. "You think I thought she was a virgin? Shit." He stood. Ruffled Rick's hair.

Rick dumped his head in his folded knees. Spilled scotch on the bed spread. He patted the wet spot into the sheet with his palm. *I should have known,* he thought. In the Vietnam logger Dan had bragged about the boat his daddy bought, a twenty-eight-foot Century Venturer. He swooned about the bikini-clad blondes as they sipped sunshine and martinis, and made fish-sucking lip gestures as they smiled at him. I had more than one, he chortled.

"Come on! So we both knew Candy. No reason to hate each other. No reason not to trust me. I never talked about Buckner. Never will. Come. Let's go," Dan stretched his hand to Rick.

Rick's hands were wet from wiping at the spilled scotch. He'd never had anyone to clean up his messes. He dried his hands on the pillowcase. He knew Dan had never worried about cleaning up anything.

Chapter **20**
Homecoming
Iguanas: Night warns iguanas to return to homes in foliage or burrows

Jesus lost his blonde along with his will to expect truth or love or escape from those who came to his homeland to feast on cheap red snapper and to sip maragritas. On his buttocks he frogged across the sand near the pier as he looked for the blonde's footprints. Velas Vallarta? He remembered her swooning of home. Shouldn't have lit the joint. What had come between them? Lungs ached as he remembered the burn of the drag. Tease. He knew then and now all about the tease of fancy shoes he had wiped clean of vomit. She would not remember he had saved her from Andale's predators. Juanita save me.

Jesus stood. He would not weep for having lost the blonde from el Norte. His life. This life. All life was here. Never again would he retreat to the Malecon to listen to the waves splash, to gaze at the childish sculpture of couples gazing out to sea. He listened. Listened to a voice singing a Spanish love song. Never having heard such sweet sound he turned his eyes inward. It is Juanita's song. Sensations of a being swelling into a fiesta celebrating his sense of self overwhelmed him. No more dreams of fleeing into space. No more dreaming. He would go on to yet this day and many more to a third job to make enough pesos to live comfortably with his dreams of making this life his.

He rubbed his hands to loosen the sand. Wiped his buttocks. It was a short beach walk from the pier to the Tropicana. He was a good waiter and even if the Americans and Canadians were not known to be big tippers, they were polite. Food-fat and friendly, they often bought buckets of beer and wimpy nachos. By mid-afternoon the burn-wary would slip under *palapas* and settle into beach novels and naps. *I can be the bold character they will take home with them in their dreams.*

Jesus changed from street clothes in the space where beach chairs and umbrellas were stored behind the wrought iron fence walling off the Tropicana from the beach. Even in his haste he remembered to turn to the Lady of Guadalupe. He crossed himself. Our Lady knew he had received the host form Padre Jose. He smiled. Absolved. Washed of the *Velas Vallarta's* sins he felt cleansed for this new day.

In the newly thatched Tropicana restaurant Jesus washed his hands in water he would not serve. Crisp in new-waiter whites he stood erect before the morning chef. Soon he was summoned to deliver a single cup of coffee. He added a pot in hopes that it might bring a bigger tip. Cups brought nothing. *Gringos!* Sometimes they like a cup on a tray. *Gringos* ordering one cup of coffee on a tray! He would not spit spite into the brown brew even though he had lost his faith in blondes. Even so, he prayed for her safety whenever he paused to think of how *Velas Vallarta* might have become what he had dreamed.

He knocked. She opened. Eyes and mouths favored escape.

Candace flicked eyes from Chase to the brown-eyed waiter. Her lips curled to cover her dismay. "Oh my god." She threw her arms around Chase. Hurtled him backward into Jesus. Coffee christened air and hair. Chase wiped the heat from his forehead. Jesus cupped hands to ears to erase the sound of crashing tray and splintering crockery.

"Here!" Candace thrust a 50-peso note to Jesus. Their eyes met. His held hers. She wiped her forehead with the back of her hand, tossed a smile to him, hoping he would catch it and leave.

"Gracias."

"So sorry, senora-ah-rita," Jesus whispered.

"Mom?" Chase peeled his eyes as he bent to reconstruct the pieces of broken cup.

"Don't, darling. Leave it for the help."

Chase kicked the door closed, leaving the mess of cup shards and coffee on the floor. He was accustomed to others cleaning up messes. "Mother!"

Candace collapsed in a fluff of fabric onto the bed. Wrist across her forehead as if suffering from a migraine, she crooked and waggled her index finger.

Chase came to her. Sat on the bed's edge. Put his hand on her knee. Leaned his head against hers. "Guess I got the wrong room." He pulled away from her. "What are? What are you doing here?"

"Sweetheart. What are you doing here? You should be in Aruba," she said before the reality of Emily's disappearance exploded in her consciousness. She began to cry.

"Don't. Don't do that. Don't."

"Hold me," she said.

Chase stood. "You followed us here. You should be ashamed." He folded his hands prayerfully to his forehead. "Same hotel? But how? How could you know?"

"Emily."

"That makes no sense Mother. Emily?"

"She's not here?"

"What? Why should she be here?"

"Oh. I'm so tired. She was abducted. I'm so scared."

"It's always Emily. Don't tell me she's run again? My god. She's twenty. Will she ever grow up? I hoped that the nuns would help her mature." He lifted his eyes to the ceiling.

Candace stretched her arms to him like the Virgin summoning the Child. Her smile was beatific.

When Chase was a child he had always scampered to her arms. Scraped elbows, bloody noses, school report cards he had hidden from Dad, he offered all for her affection. From middle school pimples to swim losses and Prom rejections, she held him. Now he was embarrassed. "Emily? Look under the bed. She's probably there. Is Father here too?"

Candace stretched her arms to him. "No. No. Listen. He's not here. You're here. We're here. And we have to find her."

He grasped her shoulders, something he had never done. "She's always done this. And," he hesitated, "and she's always had her way. I have a wife. And we need to find our way." He turned to the door. "You have a husband. Call him."

Candace spread imploring arms. Filled her face with droop of lip. "Honey?"

Door clattered shut. Candace slammed her fist into palm. "Damn. Damn. Damn all of them." She collapsed on her bed. Lifted her frantic eyes to the balcony. *Today is more of the same,* she breathed into her mind's vacuum. *Always me. Never them. All wrapped in their cocoons of privilege.* Dan's family insisted on a winter wedding. There would be more Minneapolis and Saint Paul newspaper press coverage on the society pages during the winter where they would describe her, Eyota's small-town beauty, the C-M mogul's queen dressed in a DaVinci taffeta gown with halter straps, bodice with asymmetrical pleated panel ornamented with beaded embroidery matching neckline motif, button trim back zipper, with caught-up A-line skirt extending into chapel length train strode majestically into the Cargill-Maximillian fortunes. She felt victorious. She had risen above all—until now.

Dan and Rick taxied to the Tropicana. Dan showed his identification and asked for his wife's room number.

"Oh. Oh my god," Candace fell back from the door. "Thank god."

Dan rushed to catch her, fearing that she would stumble backward, trip, snap her head on the tile floor.

She folded her eyes around all that had happened. "Emily's," she whispered as she fell.

Dan caught her.

Stunned, Rick stepped backward into the hall. *She'll never recognize me. Too long ago. Beautiful now as when she had stood beside the bus, hands on hips, posing.*

Rick smiled. Turned eyes, twisted head toward his toes in sweaty embarrassment.

Hayfield's school bus blew diesel smoke as it surged into the black night. Rick leaned his head on the back of the most remote seat, as far away from buddies, coach and driver as possible. His groin ached with sight of the beautiful blonde outside the window. He closed his eyes. Imagined her as a centerfold. Cupped his hands over his erection. Ran his mind's fingers and lips over imaginings. Bouncing headlights intruded. Knees bent backward on a bus seat, he peered from the rear emergency door. Headlights blinded him. She? He. Thumb up. Headlights flicked.

Feigning stomach cramps, a symptom all recognized and sympathized, Candace had convinced her girlfriends she was sick. Dumping them at their homes, she slowed the car. Stopped. Disconnected the odometer cable. Thank god for good-buddy footballers for their advice. Their Daddies and hers could never know the miles they had abused and would continue to abuse. She followed the bus at a distance that would not attract attention. The moment when she fumbled fingers across Chicago's WLS radio's signal, the bus lumbered into the school lot. She parked.

Turned off ignition but not WLS. She slumped. Turned up the ebbing and flowing sounds of "I Can't Help Myself."

Last to exit the bus, Rick peered to the rear before moving forward.

She flashed her bright lights.

Rick flew to the light. Through blurred eyes he stared into the face of his centerfold dreams. Her lips quivered as she rolled the window. Sweeping his fingers across his lips he touched fingers to her lips. In haste to enter he banged his shin against the car's bumper. He slid into the passenger seat. Candace shifted into drive.

Candace struggled to stand. Grasped Dan's hips as a guide. "Emily. Emily I don't know what to do."

"I'm here, Candy. I'll call. Call. Yes. I'll call Thorpe. Can't trust anyone here to help. He'll know what to do."

"Thorpe?" Candace stood. Smoothed her hair with the back of her hand.

"You still retaining him? After all that happened?" Candace had accused him of spending too much time with Sandy Thorpe before the divorce.

Dan sat with her on the bed. Folded his arms around her. "Candy. Relax. What did you fight about this time?"

"Don't. Don't say that. This is different. This is Mexico. It's totally uncivilized. I know she was abducted. We had breakfast. She wanted to go to the flea market. I didn't feel well, so I went back to the Tropicana." Candace pursed her lips and shook. "I didn't hear from her until the call."

"What call?" Dan had grown accustomed to Candace's exaggerations and Emily's willfulness.

"Emily. Emily called and said Mom. Then all I heard were distant voices."

"Candace. Stop. She's playing games. What did you fight

about? Maybe she just wanted some time to herself."

"No."

"You need air," Dan said as he helped her to her feet.

Candace leaned to steady herself as Dan guided her to the balcony. Pushing aside the billowing sheers with his left hand, he led her to air. Rick folded his arms. Joined them. A startled gecko scurried up the concrete wall.

Barry swallowed the remains of margarita. Sick with angst of Blue Beaches and losing Manny, he fell onto a blue chaise. When he awoke hours later, he coughed. Throat dry, he rubbed his chin stubble. Stood. Scratched. Stumbled through lose sand toward the Tropicana. *Oh, my god, my head. My aching head. Head. Head home. No one there. Emily? What the hell? What the hell happened? Gone. Vanished. Bad, bad move to dress her as a boy. Shouldn't have called her Manny. Manny Money. No Father help for me. Her Big Daddy might help us.*

He stumbled on a coconut shell. *Damn.* Bent foot to knee. Rubbed big toe. Folded body to the sand. Sat half-lotus. Facing the Tropicana, he looked up and saw three standing on the balcony. A male with folded arms stood behind a blonde and a big man.

"I love you," Candace said to Dan as Rick's eyes snared hers.

Sleeve to mouth, Barry wiped lips and chin clean. With blurred eyes he glanced toward the pier. Empty Corona buckets lined the pier's concrete edge. A fisher in waders stood waist-deep. He tossed a small throw-net, laying it out like a huge mariachi hat. He came up empty more often than the brown pelicans. Barry yearned for Emily, Miramar, bed and yesterday. Blue Beaches. Emily leaving with an old guy. Queen's little blond conquest scrolled across vision. He shook his head. Maybe Queen would finally be content, at least for this night, and if he barked loud and long enough, his blond might stick.

Turning his head from pier to Tropicana, Barry was startled
by the early morning figures on the balcony. Sun illuminated
Tropicana's newly painted exterior in ferocious white. Two faces
bobbed above bodies. *He, my God forgive me for calling him, my
God, he's come. And there, he stands.* Barry's stomach tightened.
He coughed, gagged.

Rick squinted. A figure squatted in the sand. Dan and
Candace parted the curtains and returned to the room. Rick
gripped the concrete slab of balcony railing and leaned forward.
The boy-man moved toward the locked gate separating Tropicana
property from public beach. He disappeared beneath a *palapa*.
Climbed over the wrought iron gate and leapt down.

Barry leaned his back against the thatched bar next to the
gate. Slumped on the concrete bar stool. He knew it was his dad
standing on the balcony. Why would he come here? Why had
he and Emily planned and plotted. "Grow up," Dad had said.
"I'll pay you back." Barry knew he couldn't. Couldn't pay back.
Couldn't grow up. He'd found Emily. Chase found his Kellie.
Now he'd lost Emily. Plot of retribution and money vanished.

Rick knew the drooping of shoulders as they sank into the
same shudder of defeat he had seen played over and over again
from Barry. Rick felt shame rise within him. Felt his hand
striking that adolescent face for shaming him when he failed to
make the swim team in eighth grade. Kid had no whiskers! Rick
wanted him to be a man.

Rick was a brute when he returned to the world from Vietnam.
How to live without fear? How to live with knowing Dan held
his life in his hands as a court martial witness? Dan. Dan the
only one who knew he had fragged the Lieutenant. Dan, the one
he hated and loved ever since Buckner spewed the venomous,
"Get the fuck out of my world." Mississippi Mudman's chunk of
flesh surfaced in Rick's day reveries and night dreams—dreams

he could neither control nor dispel with the simple suggestions of a V.A. shrink. His stomach churned. He tasted Mudman's blood in his throat. He squeezed his sphincter. What do I need? Peace. Peace son. Peace Sharon. Peace Dan. Peace Vietnam. If not peace, a cease fire.

Warmth of Rick's hand on his shoulder nearly brought tears. He couldn't remember if Dad had ever touched him lightly. Neither had ever cried.

"Here. Come with me. You can wash up."

"Dad."

Too many nights without physical comfort nicked Barry's thoughts. He hungered for peace. Seeking peace in his father's eyes Barry remembered. He bowed his head, remembered, how he lay in bed dreaming of the warmth of Father's cheek mingled with the pungent odor of sweat. He prayed that what he heard from this room above theirs was not hurting her. Whispers. Muffled shrieks. Something knocking the wall. He pressed his ear to the floor register. It was then that his mother's shrieks frightened him.

Fathers and sons can be as cold blooded as iguanas. Seeking warmth in the treetops and rooftops of the southern hemisphere iguanas have adapted to a world where warmth comes from the sky. Humans are not reptiles. Too many homosapiens are not armed with warm-blooded touch. Alpha males, taught and nourished by fathers, dominate male and female. Males often steal off-springs' souls.

"Barry."

Hands on his cheeks, hands forcing his face upward, shutting his eyes and ears to the day he was afraid not to enter, he covered his hands over those harsh imprints on his cheeks. Hands helped

Barry to rise unsteadily. A whispered, "Barry," caressed his ear. Hands withdrew. Eyes met.

Sometimes there is forgiveness. Sometimes the father drops his guard. Sometimes the son offers his ego as a sacrifice to reconciliation. This time a dog barked. Father and son stood arms around shoulders and looked toward the sound.

A she morning jogger ducked under the low tide beneath the pier. Tethered to her, a mastiff slogged behind her, its slobbering tongue hanging loosely from its flopping jowls. She looked back at him after they crossed under the bridge. "Courser! Come!" she barked. The mastiff defiant. Lips bull-stiff. Ears hanging. Exhausted. She had tied the leash around her waist without thinking that Courser would ever disobey a command. Flipped and flopping like a turtle on its back she lay on her back. Courser, as if forgiving her for her attempted dominance, licked her face.

Barry and Rick burst into laughter as they watched.

"Dad?"

"Huh?"

"Can you help me?"

"What?"

"The phone call. It was not a joke."

Rick led the way through the nearly vacant lobby, no desk clerk to be seen. They entered the tiny elevator that felt cramped when four people rode it.

Rick's eyes narrowed. "Not a joke? What?"

"Stop," Barry slipped his arm over Dad's shoulder. "I, I need you," the words sticking in his dry throat. He coughed. "I need you to help find Emily."

"Emily?"

"Yes. Lost her last night. Trouble. I love her. Don't care. Don't care about her father's money. Care. Care only her safety. She's gone." Barry looked for forgiveness.

Chapter **21**

Mismaloya

Iguanas: Are not close.

ow to bring humans close when they have fallen so far from the stars and moons that begot them? Tales of lost chances at loving and living lay like ships wrecked by maelstroms of pride, prejudice and meanness. Tomorrow's clouds shadow the plain talk of those who would dare to speak truth. Fearing too much light, humans retreat to comfort of self and unforgiveness. Iguanas bask in sun for survival. Humans cower in shade to avoid the light.

Sharon unraveled the twisted sheet between her legs, tossed it and turned to embrace the cold of an unslept pillow. She coughed. Cleared her eyes of sleep with the back of her hand. Rick should have called. Nearly noon in *Puerto Vallarta*. Same time zone as Central or was it Eastern? Eleven? Had she slept until eleven, twelve? Did it matter? Exhausted. Her mind stumbled over her unknowing. Stomach churning, she reached for the bedside table. Swigged a slug of Pepto Bismol. It did not relieve her anxiety. Wanting never to rise to this day, she cramped.

Caught between knowing and not had driven her to and from Rick in the years since Barry's birth. She chose to un-remember what had overwhelmed her. St. Paul Hotel. Executives. Private suites. Big tips. She, needing a second job, had hired on with Strictly Gourmet, Saint Paul's finest caterer. Roommate Dawn had warned her that working for such a classy caterer was dangerous.

"They might expect you to do things," she said as she turned her head away.

"Oh, Dawn. You are way too dramatic and too protective of me. But I love you for it."

The job turned Sharon into the bed of Dan whose hyphenated name was something too long to remember. His good looks and champagne charm lured her into serving him a nightcap in his private suite. She was not naive. Dawn would argue otherwise. Dawn would probe for details. Sharon would neither embellish nor reveal. "Help me uncork the Perrier Jouet," Dan smiled. "And please, bucket it on the bedside table."

The 254-room St. Paul Hotel had recently been redesigned, restored to its European elegance that enticed guests to imagine they had once slept with royalty in Vienna's Schonbrunn Palace's mini-version of Versailles. Dan tilted his head toward the turned-down bedspread. "Strangers in the Night" played softly. Exchanging a glance with Sharon, Dan plucked from a silver tray a chocolate-covered strawberry coated in a sugary-chocolate tuxedo and offered it to her lips. A silver bucket gleamed beside the bed. Room service would not disturb their champagne.

Sharon fought her sense of self and possibility of being independent with the succulent lure of an elegance she had never known. Lips soft and demanding pursued fingers offering the chocolate strawberry. Dizzy with champagne bubbles, she lay back on raspberry taffeta sheets as the strawberry nuzzled her lips.

Dan's mother had schooled him in life's nuances, but she could not protect him from the Selective Service or life's condom-less consequences. "Always order raspberry or maroon taffeta sheets," she had admonished. "And carry a condom or two in your wallet." He obeyed the former.

Morning came and he excused Sharon with a flick of his hand and twist of sheet as he rolled and turned his back to her.

Dan glanced around Candace's room. Rick and Barry entered through the unlocked door. "Rick?"

"My son, Barry," Rick said as he closed the door.

Dan's thoughts were racing. It seemed as if he hadn't heard Rick. "Candace believes Emily has been abducted." He stood with his back to the patio doors. "We need help. Calling the police is not an option."

Rick dropped his eyes to the floor and raised them to Candace. She stared at Barry.

Dan rang the hotel operator and gave her Thorpe's home phone number.

"Damn it! My daughter's missing and you can't tell me where the hell where my lawyer is? I need to talk to him right now." Dan shouted his anger at the housekeeper.

"I am sorry sir, but."

Dan cut her off. "Sorry doesn't mean crap to me, lady. You give me Thorpe's number or his monthly corporate and private retainer are gone. And. Listen very carefully. You screw this up! You go back to Mexico. *Comprende*?" He pulled Candace close to him, whispered, "Have to get legal. Sorry."

"I love you," she said as Rick's eyes snared hers.

Rick dismissed her with a blink and turn of his head.

"Yes," Dan said. "On vacation? At his condo? Mexico? Address? You got an address and a phone number?" He sat on the bed. "What? What? You say the number and address are red? Red meaning what?" He paused as he tried to suck in his anger. "Private? What? I don't give a damn! Private? You give me that number. This is Daniel Cargill-Maximillian! Got that? Thank you." He reached for a pen on the bedside table, wrote 147 Playa Cove Condominiums, Mismaloya, Jalisco 555-262-9966.

Dan told everyone to sit down. He looked skeptically at Candace, and motioned to Rick and Barry, "We're going to Thorpe's in Mismaloya." He hoped to appease Candace by seeking advice from Thorpe while at the same time assuming that Emily would be back at the Tropicana when they returned. Another of her little escapades resolved.

"Barry!"

"Yes,' Barry replied as he stood entangled in the billowing patio sheers.

"We're going to Mismaloya now. Go down to the desk and have them ring Chase. Here. He scribbled the address on a second piece of paper. If Chase isn't in his room, put this in his mail box. Tell him that's where we'll be for a couple of hours."

Barry did not want to see Chase again. Not after their encounter on the beach. And Kellie? He feared that she might think he had followed them to Mexico. All he could mutter was, "Okay."

"I'm hiring a private car. Taxi can't hold all of us," Dan said. "Meet us on the street."

Chapter 22 The Dog Barks

The iguana-she: Awakens to the cool warmth of the morning sun. Her cold blood knows no reason. Instincts do not emote. She would cover her eyes and recover her sense of her place among the natural habitat. Few humans can.

Thorpe cringed at the knock. Athena barked. Emily curled into a swooning repose on the couch. Threw the back of her hand across her forehead, a gesture she recalled from Marilyn Monroe films.

"Whoa. Ha. Wha. . . ." Thorpe fell back on his heel. Athena growled. Retreated to nuzzle Emily's hand as it fell.

Justice Thorpe justice be damned. He's quirky. Eccentric. Gay or Bi I don't care. Scared? Yes. He's damned scared I will expose him. I don't care about that. No one will ever squeeze me into submission. Thorpe, Father, Mother, Holy Ghost, no one. I am the one who obeys myself.

Dan blustered through the door. Puffing. *Too many here. He fragged while I watched the coward in me. Had he Candace before I knew she was all I ever wanted? She climbed to reach even more than I would ever be. Rick will tell more than I will. His will is more than mine. It is always winter where I live. I swear to toast eternally for the status Rick achieved that I was too cowardly to do nothing other than watch. Scotch soothed.*

Should never have called Rick little man. He rises above my stooping. He took us to the brink of courts martial. At the gate I see today forever-fallen face. He did not come when I called to him through the winter storm. My best man, little man, best man I could never be to him. Scotch never scorches me like him. Little bitch of a man climbed into my psyche. Dumps our past into the prism I have tried crushing in the chaotic corners of my dreams. Easy. It would have been too easy when I walked out of Fort Ord's gate. Easy to hug Rick. Hustle him into a ride with me into the corporate world where we would share offices. Had I never bought him a beer—none. None of this would be. Now, entangled in hopes, regrets, distrusts and imagined real or unreal truths, we burst into this room to rescue a daughter, a daughter who huddles with a dog—both safer than any of us has ever been.

On broken heel Candace stumbled into Rick. He caught her. She peered into his face. "Emilee!" she screeched.

Emily faked an abrupt awakening, forced her face to portray wide-eyed, complete and utter bewilderment. "Mother? Dad?"

"Thorpe! What the hell is Emily doing here?" Dan charged across the room. Fist-made, he cocked his arm in the ready position. Flares lit the night Rick had fragged Bruckner. He summoned Rick's anger—infused it with a stunning sense of righteousness.

Leaping to her feet, Emily wiped hair from her forehead. She jumped between her father and Thorpe. Athena barked and growled. Barked again.

"Stop! Listen to me. I was scared last night. Someone grabbed me on the beach. I ran."

When I came back with the beer, Emily was gone," Barry was bewildered by her story, but he was quick to sense she hadn't been hurt. "I thought she was mad at me for some reason and had gone to the Tropicana. I went back to the party." He put his arm around her.

"Dad I ran until my lungs ached and I collapsed."

"You lie. Why are you here!."

Rick stood beside Barry and Emily. Turning inward he could taste Dan's anger. Odor of the warm ooze of Mudman's flesh rose once again. He wanted to be a child. Wanted to be held. Wanted to be enfolded in any arms that would reach out to him. He gulped as he tried to swallow remembered anger. His eyes teared when he looked at Barry and Emily. *Emily could be the child I never had. Barry is. Barry I love. Even. Even if Sharon made me warm in the snow. Sharon never told. Never told me. Never told me I was her first. I never asked, but I felt. St. Paul Hotel, she once said. I covered her mouth with a kiss. She. Sharon saved me. From freezing she saved me. I give her roses. Our Barry's eyes are explosions. I see in them shrapnel. Dan called me little man before I killed. Remorse no. Never. Shovel the explosion of heart I could not keep alive in my hand into a body bag below the rim. A fragment of boot. I died. I thought I killed the hate. Now. Dan. Best man for his woman? No. Warmth in snow made me a man. Man. Barry. My future and he man enough now to be a father. Candace. Your eyes run into mine. Sharon's are brighter. A limo swallowed and spewed Dan. She held me to her breast. I tasted the future. Your Dan scripted your future. But tonight I planted a grenade in his tight little psyche. He drinks Glenfiddich. Tries to get into my head. I won't let him in ever again. Barry knows. I see it in his eyes. We survive. On the beach he survived whatever happened last night. Rose up from the sand. To your Dan I say I have no need to carry any of this. I know you. I see in Barry's eyes he is mine. We are armed for the future. Emily and Barry have armed themselves against destruction.*

"Thorpe! You here with my daughter. For Chrissakes. She

lies. What are you two trying to cover up?"

"Stop," Emily said calmly. "Crazy. This is crazy. He rescued me from the street and brought me here." *I know who I am. Green ants be damned. This is where Jesus left me after he found me. Thank god for that. Barry. Queen. Me. Here. I always ran. Stunned all of them. I out-ran the she-they-wanted-me-to-be. Thorpe? Scared. Blue Beaches. Couldn't out-run him. Café de Olla. Mother feigning outrage. Bleeding me. Sting of fingernails. Running? Now running to. Barry. Everyone let go of me. Barry. Hold me.*

Knocking roused Athena's ferocious bark. Emily patted Athena. "It's okay, girl." Athena whimpered and plopped at Emily's feet.

Barry bent down to pet Athena. *Chase brought Kellie here where it is best not to have a name. This can be home for Emily and me. It will if we will. Will they fish for answers to the calls? Why the hell did we call? Why? Extort money? Calling Dad was stupid. Necks in a noose. I look. Queen discovered his blonde. Chase closes eyes and arms around Kellie. We explored each other. Found it lacking. No imploring looks like those filling this room with angst. Will our lives ever rise to resolve dreams? I know I need Emily. Chase needs Kellie. Swim-slaps on the ass invigorated our spirits. My sprints ached all through college for images of Chase's conquests. He the hero—excluded me from his family circle. I never understood why. Me, the hired pool boy. Filters. I knew more than she thought I knew. What if I had bought and brought the filters? Enter Chase's mother's bed? Tease. Emily is not a tease*

Chase and Kellie stepped through the door. Chase stared in disbelief as he saw Emily and Barry petting and calming the dog. *Barry here? Too many here. Our honeymoon and all here. How could they have known. I told everyone we were going to Aruba. We came here to escape. Saint John's walls bricked me in. Forever connected me to brothers until Kellie's touch. Abbot Paul. His face rises. Father Ambrose admonishes. Never send a brother to the woods alone with an axe. A man could send his soul to heaven with one misplaced stroke. Tangled in sheets from a guilty past I find peace in her. Barry. I will never regret the who-we-were there, then on the banks of Stumpf Lake. I knew future began and ended there on the bridge when we pissed and fell. Swam to warmth of a shore where wood would warm us. Two fires burned within me. Like two roads in one of Father Ambrose's late night chats. He loved Robert Frost. The evening he escorted me to the Saint John's woods—told me to sit beside him on a log where the path forked. It was the night of my sophomore year after I had flunked a calculus exam. Cold and distance between us. Look, he said. Which way will you go? I didn't understand. You choose, I remember him saying. You choose and God will follow. He put his hand on my shoulder. Son, he said. It is time for you to choose. You will make of your life what is best for you. Here, these honeymooned nights I learned that I can love in many ways while I know he and she will love me.*

Candace fluffed her hair with a dramatic twist of her palm. *Dan, Rick creeping into me without knowing. Neither knowing the living I loved without them. It began in Eyota. The hardware store. I knew then what I could do to men. I felt lust flowing from men and boys even then. Ever fearing yet hoping that love would waft me away from the littleness of that town, I knew I could outrun any of them who would chase me. It was then that I knew if ever I had a son, I would name him Chase. I would teach him not to chase after dreams that evaporate as soon as one awakens to the lightning always-lurking thunder-seconds beyond the horizon. Hour with Rick—Dan will never know. The cheering of the crowd when I swung legs high over hurdles urged me to run. Run. I outran all men except two. Pool. Curl of lip. The bulging boy. Chase begged me to hire him. I know. I wanted him. Chase knew him? How? No. Not knowing him in that way. But maybe? Chase is a chaser. I will survive all but Emily. She is truth. I lost mine. She seizes now. Stop. She's stopped. Barry. Barry stopped her. Never know. Never. Never know what I was before he was your father. Money saved me from falling. Falling into a poverty of spirit I knew I could not endure. Once? Once when? Before I became a queen? A trophy. Poverty of romance. Until that night. They come together here. Daddy will kill Rick if . . . . No. There will be no knowing. I fill my life of was that never could be. Life now. Now I will give all of myself to. To pray. To say peace.*

"Stop!" Emily shouted. "All this chasing and mistrust has to stop." She pointed at Athena. "She is wiser than any of you."

Chase drew Kellie closer to him.

Barry put his arm around Emily's waist. Squeezed her so tightly that she gasped. Athena whimpered.

Jesus stepped into the dark as he waited for the bus to take him home. *Juanita speaks to me in dreams. I have not listened. Ship's lights in nights across Bandaris Bay lured me. Our Lady of Guadalupe's majestic glow and ringing stung my senses in the midnights I stood looking up to the stars and to the sculptures pointing to heaven. Always pointing north. I dreamed of blondes, the dreams of the blonde from el Norte were so close I could have captured them and made them real. But Juanita always called me home. Home to our Puerto. Our Vallarta. Always she came to me in the night. Folded her arms around me. Entangled me in her flowing hair. "Listen," she whispered. "Listen to who we are. We are mejicanoamejicana. I wanted to love and live Emily.*

"Listen to who we are. Be proud. Be here where food is love, love offered from the souls of your mother's and her ancestors' dreams. Respect. Respect our royalty." Juanita smiled.

Iguanas: have many, many special care needs. When those needs are not met, iguanas will suffer in many ways. It is important to give iguanas all the recommended care to help them thrive in captivity.

Humans: have many, many special care needs. When those needs are not met, humans suffer in many ways. It is important to give humans all the recommended care to help them survive their captivity.

Angstron's Jay

A Short Story

Wind scattered snow and flecks of sparrows from the sill. Louise dropped a pan over my head, rattling the light fixture. Books were poisoned flies scattered across my desk. A half chapter there, back up, raw and unread, blinked in grayed lamplight. Teaching was good, but I had to quit before we strangled each other with boredom. Kids, adolescents, immortals, Kafka, Lowell, Shakespeare all spread before me in confusion. Trying to read all evening, I came out empty.

Louise worked. I ground fingernail grist with my teeth. Stored it in the ashtray. Sparrows had taken over the martin house. I should have cleaned them out. No martin anyway, just sparrows and jays, screeching. I couldn't take the screeching. In the hours since dusk it had come inside, echoing, recoiling and bursting, strafing every minute. I was alone, puncturing and deflating them so nothing was left by hollowness.

"Raymond! Your egg is ready."

You mean yours, dear? Would you like it fertilized? I couldn't eat another egg. We just had them for supper, scrambled. My God, wouldn't that woman ever learn about cholesterol? It had already clogged the veins in my penis. Wasn't that enough? How could she know? She didn't know I wasn't working.

"Sparrow!" I shouted through the cold air return. Furnace

149

kicked in. My gut twisted. Even in the middle of night, that noise was like a razor blade slicing the inside of my elbow. I hadn't slept the night through since October for worrying about the dollar bills burning.

"Coming!" I yelled, swallowing a fingernail. "And turn the damn thermostat down. There's less than an eighth tank left." Of course she wouldn't hear me, but I'd said it anyway. Robert Lowell's *Lord Weary's Castle* in hand, I climbed the basement stairs. Thought I'd read "Skunk Hour" so Louise would leave me alone.

"Which Mass are we going to? We should go early, you know," she said, ignoring me and the book. She talked to the butter. "Skunk Hour" would be more comfortable than this. I stared back at the egg.

"You go," I said. "Swipe me a wafer and I'll commune at brunch."

"Raymond! Stop it. You can't talk like that." I felt her eyes pecking. "We have to go. I promised the Melons we'd have brunch."

I poked the yoke with my fork. Watched the yellow ooze into the pockmarks of the toast. Reminded me of George sliding into Elaine. Six little Melons for Chrissakes, and the probably weren't through yet. I think George was trying to grin and screw his way into the state senate. Wanted to prove to the voters he isn't gay. I'd have bet he prayed that they'd forgotten he was Vietnam hawk, the son of a bitch.

"Call them," I said. "I'm sick."

"You know I can't do that. They're in bed."

"And their bodies are entwined like vines at the pearly gate." I laughed.

Louise stabbed the butter, opening a gash that would have bloodied the entire table. "You're ridiculous, Raymond," she said calmly, but her eyes were skinned. "I won't call them. And we will go. We will go to ten o'clock Mass. I'm going to bed."

The egg was dying. I listened to the furnace struggle against the cold. It breathed more easily than I. Bedroom door stood cracked open. Toilet flushed reassuringly. Limbs of light speared the carpet. I wanted to wade toward them, to be pulled by their pinkness into a nest where the screeching would stop. The limbs snapped black. Blue Jays slept. I shivered, awake in the storm. Ought to have made a fire. But I had cut the wood green, four weekends I cut, split, hauled, ached for wood that wouldn't burn. Louise had laughed at me then.

"George ages his wood," she had said. "They're always warm."

"Turn on the goddamn electric blanket then. That'll keep your warm." She knew I couldn't sleep with that damn red light glowing.

"What?" Louise's voice intruded from the black.

"Nothing. Nothing. Go to sleep, Louise."

"Are you coming to bed?"

Turn on the lights, Louise. Warm lights. Not red. Tell me Randy's home. Then the storm will stop. We'll make it stop. Together. In the light. I'm cold. My legs are black marble. Cold. All of cold. They have dates marking their cooling. The Angstrons. Mother first. Dad. Randy. Taps. Screeching. I won't go there anymore. It's windy. Cold. Their marble is black.

"No. I'm not coming to bed." My teeth jumped; knee chattered against my hand. Wind rode branches to exhaustion, spraying snow lather on trees' twisted wounds. Reflected in the window, the last lighted lamp in our house pulsated. Iced power lines, reflecting from the yard light, sliced silver light through the black. Soon they'd snap. We shouldn't have built in the country. Louise had always feared being powerless. We have light. A candle. In the loft bedroom. Randy's room. He had sent it from Saigon. "In case the lights go out—again," he had written.

"You really should buy a kerosene lamp. Or candle at least, Ray."

Yeah, little brother. You're right. But the lights have never gone out before. More?" I asked, already pouring whiskey into his Coke.

"In basic training they turned the lights out at nine. I used to write letters in the latrine. Man, did my ass get cold," he laughed and drank.

"No ladies to warm it either, right?" I liked to watch Randy grin. His whole face exploded.

"Right. But I got crabs anyway," his eyes flickered. He winked.

"You two," Louise said. "I'm glad Ray is too old to be drafted. Crabs. Ugh." She shivered voluntarily, making music with ice in her glass. She was beautiful then. We were quiet, warm. I could taste the three of us together, the last of the Angstrons. The electrical power had been out all night but it didn't matter.

"Ray?" His voice as low and cold like the wind in the corner of a snowstorm.

Don't. Not now, Randy. We're almost through the night. Don't.

"I won't die." His eyes went far away into the ice regions. I tried to follow but he turned his head into the shadows. Lightning cracked, exploded, spraying our bodies with the blue-gray terror. Louise gasped. I looked to reach for her hand. She folded her arms like a broken-winged canary, turned into the shadows and cried. They were bucket riders. Smoke backed out of the fireplace, circled Randy's head. I wanted to breathe it away from him but I was too cold.

"Don't go," I said. "We'll go to Canada. We'll go to

Winnipeg. The three of us. I can teach there. And you can go to college. Winnipeg isn't far. Only a few hundred miles. What do you say?"

"No," he said, as he withdrew from the shadows. "I'm a medic. They need me."

"No one's gotten any sleep. I'll make some coffee." Louise's shadow slid between Randy and me.

"No power. Remember?" Randy smiled.

"Yes," Louise looked at me. "And no candles either."

Crowding through the mist on the hill's edge, the sun quivered, irritating my eyes. Through a squint I saw a mourning dove, felt her coo-ah, coo warmth. "Should replace the martin house with a dove cote," I said before I realized I could be heard.

"Look!" Randy pointed for Louise to see, his other arm protecting her.

Louise's jay skimmed the dove's head, sent the swooning bird in spiraled flight toward safety.

"At least the dove survived," I said, but no one paid any attention. "Forget it. We'll get coffee at the airport. Ready?"

I felt a hand. "Come to bed, Ray. Don't sit alone in the dark." Louise rubbed my shoulder. "Listen to the wind." I felt her breath warming my neck. "Aren't you cold?"

"The power!" I jumped. "Listen. The furnace isn't running."

Louise moved away from me. I heard her hand scraping the plaster until she found the light switch. Nothing.

"What'll we do?" Louise sounded frightened. "Did you listen to the weather report?"

"No. You?"

"No. No I didn't." She had found a quilt somewhere in the dark. I felt its warmth on my shoulders.

"There." Her breath was close.

"Maybe if we had a light, I could find some wood." I knew that wasn't true, but it would keep her mind off the storm.

"No. We don't need a light. This is fine. We won't freeze. Plenty of quilts. I can phone George. He has a snowmobile. I'll ask him to bring wood." Here voices were like wires swinging in the wind. Jay. She's a jay, I thought.

"No. Just sit still. Here. Wrap the quilt around you. I'll get the candle from Randy's room." I remember reading that a candle can keep a car warm enough for people to survive.

"Ray?" the high-wired voice called behind me.

"Christ! The end table! My shin!" Shouldering the wall, I propped myself so I could rub my leg. "What? I can't hear you."

"We don't need it," she whispered. Where she had come from I didn't know but we were standing together on the stairs.

"We do, Louise. It's all there is. Don't you see!"

"I threw it out," she said softly.

"Killer!" I screeched.